Lisa's life was on the line

Nash had to make it safe for her again. He understood the evidence of the case, but the attacks were directed *at her*. He was willing to take a bullet in the line of duty, but there was no way he'd drag Lisa into the danger of his job. Inevitably, anything more than friendship would do that.

Even as Nash insisted to himself that he was restraining his feelings, that he was keeping as much distance as he could, he also knew it was a lost cause. Lisa was in his blood.

Four years hadn't changed that.

He should be smarter, he thought. A hell of a lot smarter. But he couldn't let her go. He couldn't let someone else hold her. Images of Lisa and the past they'd once shared crowded his brain.

Nash didn't think he was strong enough to let her go....

Dear Harlequin Intrigue Reader,

Beginning this October, Harlequin Intrigue has expanded its lineup to *six* books! Publishing two more titles each month enables us to bring you an extraordinary selection of breathtaking stories of romantic suspense filled with exciting editorial variety—and we encourage you to try all that we have to offer.

Stock up on catnip! Caroline Burnes brings back your favorite feline sleuth to beckon you into a new mystery in the popular series FEAR FAMILIAR. This four-legged detective sticks his whiskers into the mix to help clear a stunning stuntwoman's name in *Familiar Double*. Up next is Dani Sinclair's new HEARTSKEEP trilogy starting with *The Firstborn*—a darkly sensual gothic romance that revolves around a sinister suspense plot. To lighten things up, bestselling Harlequin American Romance author Judy Christenberry crosses her beloved BRIDES FOR BROTHERS series into Harlequin Intrigue with *Randall Renegade*—a riveting reunion romance that will keep you on the edge of your seat.

Keeping Baby Safe by Debra Webb could either passionately reunite a duty-bound COLBY AGENCY operative and his onetime lover—or tear them apart forever. Don't miss the continuation of this action-packed series. Then Amy J. Fetzer launches our BACHELORS AT LARGE promotion featuring fearless men in blue with *Under His Protection*. Finally, watch for *Dr. Bodyguard* by debut author Jessica Andersen. Will a hunky doctor help penetrate the emotional walls around a lady genius before a madman closes in?

Pick up all six for a complete reading experience you won't forget!

Enjoy,

Denise O'Sullivan
Senior Editor
Harlequin Intrigue

UNDER HIS PROTECTION

AMY J. FETZER

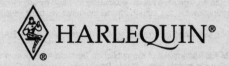

HARLEQUIN®

TORONTO • NEW YORK • LONDON
AMSTERDAM • PARIS • SYDNEY • HAMBURG
STOCKHOLM • ATHENS • TOKYO • MILAN • MADRID
PRAGUE • WARSAW • BUDAPEST • AUCKLAND

ISBN 0-373-22733-7

UNDER HIS PROTECTION

Copyright © 2003 by Amy J. Fetzer

ABOUT THE AUTHOR

Amy J. Fetzer was born in New England and raised all over
the world. She uses her own experiences in creating the
characters and settings for her novels. Married more than
twenty years to a United States Marine and the mother of
two sons, Amy covets the moments when she can curl up
with a cup of cappuccino and a good book.

Books by Amy J. Fetzer

HARLEQUIN INTRIGUE
733—UNDER HIS PROTECTION

SILHOUETTE DESIRE
1089—ANYBODY'S DAD
1132—THE UNLIKELY BODYGUARD
1181—THE RE-ENLISTED GROOM
1265—GOING...GOING...WED!*
1305—WIFE FOR HIRE*
1361—TAMING THE BEAST*
1383—HAVING HIS CHILD*
1445—SINGLE FATHER SEEKS...*
1467—THE SEAL'S SURPRISE BABY

*Wife, Inc.

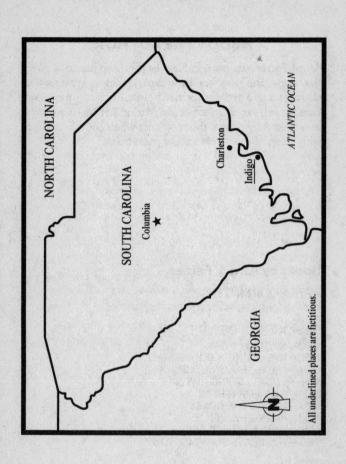

NORTH CAROLINA

SOUTH CAROLINA

Columbia ★

Charleston •

Indigo •

ATLANTIC OCEAN

GEORGIA

N

All underlined places are fictitious.

CAST OF CHARACTERS

Lisa Bracket-Winfield—Four years ago Lisa left Indigo with a painful secret she'll never reveal.

Detective Nash Couviyon—When Lisa finally comes back into his life, it's not as his friend or lover, but as his prime suspect in a strange murder.

Peter Winfield—the victim, hiding more secrets than his ex-wife ever knew.

William Reese Baylor—Owner of the Baylor Inn. Murder under his roof has cost him more than customers.

John Chartres—Baylor Inn's concierge. Does his superior attitude and attention to detail include planning the perfect murder?

Kathy Boon—A new face in town. Did what she heard and saw lead to her disappearance?

Catherine Delan—Linked to a married man, she has more to gain than anyone. And that makes her dangerous.

Carl Forsythe—Is he the killer or the key to why Winfield was murdered?

To Ronnie,
aka Kelsey Roberts

For your guidance and insight
while I stumbled through in a new genre
For pink friends,
weekends of dressing badly
and free association moments
For being friends
and mostly, for staying that way
even when things get weird

Love you, girl.

Prologue

Indigo, South Carolina

His death smelled like lavender.

Moisture from his bath still hung in the air like a veil, preventing him from sensing more than the cramping in his stomach, the flashes of hot and cold thrashing over his skin. The gradually slowing beat of his heart.

His thoughts collided, spilling into one another till he couldn't recall truth from memory, fiction from fact. The buzzing of the phone, half-off its cradle, droned like a fly. Was it day or night? He could see no more than slivers of light draped in shadows.

As he lay on the bed, a towel barely covering him, his body felt heavy, immobile, pressed into the antique quilt. He hated being helpless. He hated disorder and the vulgarity of illness. Fury worked beneath his clammy skin and he tried to use it to counter the seeping of strength from his body in thick, oppressing waves. How long had he felt this numb? Earlier he'd thought it was the flu. But he knew better. It was happening too fast. The fire beneath his skin, the furious headache that only grew stronger. His eyes shifted sluggishly, the simple effort like sand grinding behind his lids, and the room tilted, the furniture stretching like something out of a cartoon.

His heartbeat slowed, beating a painful dirge toward his death.

He tried to reach again for the phone to call for help, but his fingers only flexed with a faint spring, then went still. Regret lanced through him, and her face filled his mind. Always her. She was his wife. She always would be.

He hated being pitiful, pathetically weak. And he was. Completely. His heartbeat dropped another notch, and he couldn't fill his lungs. Saliva dribbled from his mouth and down the side of his face. He heard a noise and blinked to focus. He hadn't the strength to turn his head, and the indignity of it, the slovenliness, humiliated him.

He'd have preferred a bullet between the eyes, messy as that would be. They would find him like this, he thought. Wet, naked and in God knew what state. A shadow moved, a shape forming in the faint light.

Help! Thank God, help!

His whimper shamed him, but he was desperate. Then the figure leaned over the bed. His eyes widened, but only a fraction. Rage and confusion ground down to the marrow of his bones, and he choked on words he couldn't form, couldn't push past his lips.

Why?

His killer smiled and watched him die.

Chapter One

The damp heat of Indigo in September still clung like a bad tempered child. By eight in the morning its punishing grip was firm and hot and wouldn't be tamed till well past sunset. Locals were used to it, visitors complained about it, but that Detective Nash Couviyon had to investigate a suspicious death this early was an indecent slap to the beauty of the nearly three-hundred-year-old town.

Worse when death occurred in the richly appointed Baylor Inn, the jewel of Southern hospitality in Indigo and smack-dab in the center of the historic old town. He could almost hear the mayor's outrage at such an event occurring here and scaring the tourists.

By the time Nash had arrived at the suite, the officers had already sealed off the floor and taken photographs. Unfortunately there were no witnesses to the crime. The victim had been locked in his suite and found by a member of the housekeeping staff in the morning.

Nash took a sip of coffee from a paper cup so thin

his fingers, encased in latex gloves, felt seared by the heat. He circumvented the room again. Antique dressers bore two hundred years of wear like an ancient king. The thick down comforter on the bed reminded him of how little sleep he'd had the night before. The body of the victim was sprawled across the wide mattress.

Nash ignored it for a moment, his gaze picking through details that were not so obvious: the crystal tumbler with the dregs of a cocktail, the unopened briefcase neatly tucked under the desk. The air was filled with a revolting combination of death and the sweetness of flowers. Very little was out of place, no signs of a struggle. The sofa and stuffed chairs sat facing the hearth, and the only furniture that wasn't an antique was an armoire holding the television and VCR. Resting on the lowboy was a sweet-grass basket filled with teas, packaged snacks, flavored coffees and a china mug only a woman would use. On the basket was a small brass oval engraved with ''Enchanted Garden.'' He frowned. Enchanted Garden was a nursery his brother Temple used in his landscaping business. Nash took account of the contents and gestured to an officer, who then bagged it.

A look through the victim's clothing hanging in the closet, shoes precisely two inches apart, socks arranged by color, told Nash that the victim was fanatical about his appearance. The remains on the room-service tray from the night before indicated he cared about what he ate, too. It was so healthy it made Nash cringe.

Nash moved to the bathroom before examining the body again. His gaze sharpened at the evidence, sifting normal from unusual. The victim had bathed leisurely. His neatly arranged shaving gear and toiletries added to Nash's initial feeling that the victim was picky about order. Several candles littered the edge of the tub, burned down to the nubs and dripping into the cold, cloudy bathwater. The mess contradicted what he'd seen so far. Then he leaned over the tub to lift what looked like a large teabag out of the water. Untying the ribbon that secured the thing to the faucet, he sniffed. So that was where the flower smell came from, he thought, lowering it into the evidence bag, then marking it. He handed the bag to an officer, then left the bathroom and returned to the suite. He stopped at the foot of the bed, staring at the victim.

White male, perhaps thirty-five, naked except for a towel around his waist and the scarf wrapped around his throat. Muscular body even in death, stylish haircut, manicured nails.

"Everything tagged and bagged?" Nash asked the patrol supervisor.

"Except him," the man said, then handed him the victim's wallet as he walked past.

Absently Nash slipped the wallet from the evidence bag, yet his attention, for the moment, was on the coroner.

At the side of the bed, Quinn Kilpatrick examined

the body. His thickly muscled arms strained against his jacket sleeves, and though Quinn was built like a linebacker, he handled the body as if it were fine porcelain.

"What do you have for me?"

"You cops, always impatient." Quinn bagged the victim's hands.

"Hey, pillage and plunder, murder and mayhem, are going on as we speak. We have to go out and be heroes."

Quinn smirked, but didn't glance up as he lifted the victim's arm to look beneath. "Dead nine hours at least."

"The scarf?"

Quinn eased the nearly transparent pale-green scarf from around the victim's neck. "There are ligature marks, but they're not really dark enough to indicate this was the cause of death. Maybe postmortem. No other signs of strangulation. I'll know more when I get him into the lab." Quinn straightened, frowning still. "See this?"

"The rash?"

"It's not a rash, it's a reaction."

"He didn't have any medication, except vitamins, but he took a bath. Maybe it's from whatever he added to the water?" Nash could still smell the flowery fragrance.

Quinn started to put the scarf into an evidence bag, then frowned, smelling the fabric. He held it out to Nash, who moved near and inhaled.

"Perfume." Something caught in his gut. "That's familiar." And he knew exactly where he'd smelled the fragrance before. It was the one Lisa wore.

Lisa Bracket… Oh, hell. Lisa Bracket Winfield. His gaze snapped to the ID, then the body.

Peter David Winfield. Lisa's husband. The man she married, instead of him. Well, that wasn't quite true, he argued. Nash'd never asked her to marry him. After a year of dating steadily, he'd never told her he loved her, and when he said he didn't want to get serious, she'd ended their relationship. A few months later she was dating Winfield, and Nash, like a jerk, cut her completely out of his life like a bad-tempered high-school jock the day before the prom. Six months later she was gone. And married. But she was in town, that much he knew from Temple. Alone. So why wasn't she here with Winfield?

He flipped through the wallet, and her familiar face stared back at him from a photo. It landed a punch right between the eyes.

Lisa in her wedding dress.

He closed his eyes briefly, remembering her face with four-year-old clarity, the feel of her body against his and what she did to him with just a look. Which was plenty. His mind was latched on to the memory of her last kiss when someone called his name.

Nash, still trapped in the past, rubbed his face and looked up.

"There's a woman wanting to speak with you."

"Tell her she'll have to wait."

"I think you should talk to her, sir." The officer's gaze shifted briefly to the body on the bed. "She's the victim's wife."

Nash's features tightened, and he stepped into the hall, his gaze moving immediately to the barricade. Lisa stood beyond, an officer keeping her back.

"Nash."

If he thought the picture of her punched him in the gut, seeing her in person tore him in two. It was fast heartbeats and the need to touch her all over again. Four years had only made her more beautiful. Red-haired, green-eyed and willowy slim. And she was married.

Well, a widow.

Nash glanced inside the hotel room. Emergency medical technicians were lifting the sheet-wrapped victim into a body bag, then onto a stretcher. Pulling the door closed behind him, he motioned the officer to let her pass.

Immediately Nash ushered her away from the suite and into a room they'd commandeered for questioning potential witnesses. Once inside, he positioned a patrolman outside, then closed the door.

Lisa frowned at the way Nash was acting. She hadn't seen him in ages except for passing glimpses from a car now and then. Indigo was small compared to New York, but being on the fringes of Charleston, it was plenty large enough to get lost in. Lost enough not to have come face-to-face like this.

For a few moments they just stared at each other. "Hello, Lisa," Nash finally said.

Lisa felt her stomach lurch as his deep voice rolled over her. God, he looked good. "Hey, Nash. How's life treating you?"

Lousy, he thought, but said, "Decent. It's been a while."

This came with a hint of apology. Lisa shrugged, although her heart was hopping like a frog in a pond. "About four years, huh?"

The stiffness between them was almost palpable as Nash's gaze moved over her from head to foot. She looked bright and fresh, scrubbed healthy, her red tank top exposing tanned arms, the short denim skirt showing off her long legs. Great gams, his father would've called them. "You said you'd never come back to Indigo."

Why was he bringing this up *now?* she wondered. "Things change. I was born here. This is my home. Besides, you pushed me to say that," she said, remembering their last fight. "I was angry."

"I didn't push you anywhere. Hell, you're the one who wanted to end—"

He stopped abruptly, and she could see him shut down, close off. Typical, she thought.

He ran his hand over his mouth and sighed. "Well, that was real mature," he said sheepishly.

Yes, it was, she agreed silently, for both of them.

Coolly, he gestured to two chairs set opposite each other at a delicate Queen Anne table, and as she sat, he poured her a cup of coffee in china cups the hotel manager had set out. He added cream to hers, just the right amount, and that he remembered sent her to a strange place in her heart. She tried to leave it.

"What exactly is going on here, Nash?"

He met her gaze, his expression offering nothing. That wasn't unusual for Nash Couviyon. Except for his younger brother Temple, keeping feelings all locked inside was a family trait. She studied him, his dark hair shorter than she remembered, though the rest of him had changed little. He sat, the fabric of his suit jacket pulling against his broad shoulders as he braced his arms on the tabletop. It was hard not to notice the size of him, that the delicate cup was like a glass ornament in his fist, easily crushed. Planed like a sculptor's creation in stone, he looked deadly, unbreakable. Unshakable. The sharp line of his jaw slid unrelenting to his cheekbones, slightly hollow beneath blue eyes. Wicked blue eyes, she'd always thought. Eyes that melted her insides, yet there was no sign of softness in them now. They were glass hard. Pinning her.

She sent the stare right back at him, bracing herself against feeling anything for him. Even as she thought that, she knew it was impossible. This was Nash.

"My employee, Kate, called my cell phone," she said, "and told me the police asked me to come over, though I have no idea what for. Care to explain?"

Nash hated this part and prayed she hadn't been anywhere near her husband in the past twelve hours. "Your husband is dead."

Her expression went slack. "That's impossible."

"I'm sorry, but he's in the next room, with the coroner."

"But he was fine last night."

Oh, God. "You were with him?"

She didn't clue in to the narrow look he shot her. "I was married to him, Nash. If he was in town, don't you think we'd at least see each other?"

"But you haven't been living in the same city?"

"That's because we were divorcing. As of this morning, our divorce is final."

Nash frowned. This was not the conversation he'd thought he'd be having with her right now.

"Who do you think killed him?" she asked.

"Why would you say that?"

"I noticed the badge, Nash." Her gaze darted where it hung on his jacket pocket. "You're a detective now, not the chief coroner." She arched a brow. "And Peter was a stockbroker—he made enemies daily."

"I work on all suspicious deaths. You one of those enemies?"

"No, of course not. Peter adored me." Too much, she thought. That adoration had twisted into something ugly. "However, we've been legally separated for two and a half years."

A year after her marriage they separated? He didn't want to feel smug about that. "Legal separation before filing isn't that long. Why not divorce sooner? Why now?"

His shock didn't do a thing for her except make her

feel sick. It was tough to admit that her marriage had failed so early. "I couldn't afford to divorce him till recently, and he wouldn't do it. In fact, last night, he…oh, jeez."

For the first time it hit her, really hit her. And Nash watched as her features fell, her lower lip quivered. She looked down at the china cup, but when she brought it to her mouth, her trembling proved that her grip on her emotions was tenuous. She set the cup down.

Tears welled up in her eyes and fell. She cried without sound.

Nash ached to hold her, but he was on duty, and not one of her favorite people, so he kept his distance. She was a suspect, a prime one. She wouldn't want his help, anyway, but it was killing him to watch her fight her tears. Lisa had always been a tough cookie, and to see her come apart was heartbreaking. Teardrops hit her hands and the table in tiny plops.

He felt them like gunshots.

He left his chair and grabbed a tissue, shoving it into her line of sight. She muttered thanks and took it. It was several more minutes before she regained her composure. Nash felt useless.

"I need to ask you a few more questions."

She nodded and met his gaze, sniffling once.

Nash set a tape recorder on the table and pushed record. He recited her name, marital status, age, the time… Lisa didn't hear the rest. She was too stunned to listen. Was he questioning her as a suspect or character witness?

"For the record, when did you last see Peter Winfield?"

She blinked at the recorder, then met his gaze. "Last night at around eight-thirty, nine o'clock. He'd called me and asked me to come over."

"What happened?"

"He wanted one more chance to make me stay with him."

"Make you?"

Always a cop, she thought, reading something into every little thing. "Well, *make* isn't really correct. *Convince* would be a better word." *Threaten* would be even better.

"Why did you divorce?"

She looked down at her coffee, watching the cream separate into a star shape. "Irreconcilable differences."

"I don't buy that for a second."

Her gaze jerked to his. "It's personal." Nash wasn't getting details. No one was.

"But you left town with him so quickly."

This was old news, she thought. "It was four months after you and I had broken up, Nash. You'd already shoved me out of your life, so what do you care now?"

His mouth tightened, a lid on what he really wanted to say. "We were together for a year, and you never did give me a good reason for why you left me."

She didn't want to rehash this now. "Oh, there was plenty of reasons, they just weren't yours. I needed someone who wanted what I did." Someone to love me back, she thought. To want me for a lifetime and not just a frequent date.

"And did you get all you wanted?"

Damn him. He knew she hadn't, but that didn't mean she wasn't deliriously happy with what she had right now. It wasn't any of his business why her marriage ended, only that it had. And who was he to ask questions now when he didn't bother four years ago? If he had, she'd have told him about their baby. "Are old feelings and reasons part of this investigation, Detective?"

Nash felt the slam of a door as if it hit his nose. She was right. He had to get back to business and not relive their past.

"Did you drive over last night?" he asked.

"No, it was only just getting dark and it was a clear night. I walked."

"Did anyone see you?"

"Walking here? I imagine so. Anyone I know? I can't say. When I got here, the restaurant was full, and the staff were waiting on guests. I came up here and knocked."

"What was Winfield wearing when you saw him?"

"I beg your pardon?"

"Answer the question, please."

With the way he spoke to her, so cold and detached, as if they'd never shared a bed and some really great sex, she wondered if she should stop right now and call a lawyer. But she hadn't done anything wrong.

"He was wearing Brooks khaki slacks, matching socks. A hunter-green, tailored, short-sleeve shirt, pressed and creased. Brown Florsheim shoes and a brown belt." Good clothing had been an addiction of Peter's.

Nash made notes in a black leather book. His gaze slid up to meet hers, and for a second his expression softened a fraction. Lisa glimpsed the man she once loved. Then just as quickly that man was gone again.

"Did anyone else know you were going to see him?"

"I might have mentioned it to my staff." She wiped her eyes again, then threw the wad of tissue into a trash can.

"I'll need to talk with them."

Why? she wanted to know, but she didn't argue. "Free country. They're adults, not children. I'll give you their home numbers." She wrote the information on the back of a business card and handed it to him. He didn't even glance at it, simply tucked it in his notebook. "Kate's at the counter now, and Chris doesn't come in till after his last class. He's a college student at USC."

Nash scribbled and she noticed the shorthand. She'd flunked that course.

"What were you wearing at the time you visited your husband?"

"A lime-green skirt and top, matching sandals and purse."

He arched a brow.

"Matching jewelry, too. Wanna see it?"

"I'll want to take all of it."

"What?" Her eyes widened, and the feeling she'd had moments ago landed like a brick against her heart. "You think I had something to do with Peter's death."

Nash continued to write.

"Nash Couviyon!"

Still he didn't comment, then slowly met her gaze again. "I don't have an opinion yet. We need samples from your things to compare with what forensics finds in the room."

"You definitely think he was murdered?"

Nash wasn't ready to say so just yet. "The death of a healthy man is always suspicious."

"Oh, for the love of Mike," she said, and the air left her lungs in one shot. "You actually think I had something to do with it?"

Her words drained away any feeling she had, any trust she might have given him. Then the she-cat he remembered and had loved came racing back.

"This meeting is over," she said.

He strove for patience. "Lisa, I have to look at all the possibilities."

Her green eyes narrowed to slits. "Look elsewhere, Detective," she said, and started to rise.

"Sit down!" he snapped.

Lisa lowered herself into the chair again, scowling at him.

"It's either here or the station, Lisa. Your choice."

She folded her arms and glared. "Fine. Ask away."

"Did you carry anything into the room besides your handbag?"

Lisa searched his features. "No, but I had on a scarf."

Something inside Nash froze. "Describe it please."

"It was my grandmother's. It's pale green with hand-painted irises. It's the reason I got here so quickly this morning. I was on my way here to get it back."

"Why did you leave it?"

"I didn't. It was in my hair, which I had in a ponytail. The scarf was tied around the rubber band to hide it. It must have come undone. It's silk and slippery."

Nash wrote, the notebook sliding on the highly polished table. The business card she'd given him showed and he flipped it over.

Lisa thought she saw sadness flicker in his eyes.

"The Enchanted Garden, that's your business?"

"Yes." She frowned. "Didn't you already know that?"

Nash shook his head.

"I started it up about ten months ago. It's on my land around the house and it's doing really well." Her brows knit. "I don't get it. Your brother Temple buys some of his plants for his landscaping business from me. I thought you knew.''

"I knew he used this nursery, but he never mentioned it was yours.''

"Maybe he thought he was being disloyal to his older brother by doing business with me. I know how you Couviyon brothers stick together.''

"Obviously, Temple has his own set of rules.''

"I know, he's an outrageous flirt.''

She was trying to ease the tension in the room. But Nash could feel it thicken the air. He tossed the card down and rose, moving to the door and speaking to the officer posted outside, who moved off to do his bidding. Nash waited, glancing back at her only once. She couldn't have done this, he thought.

"Why didn't you ever come by to say hello, Nash?''

"I knew you were here, Lisa.'' He didn't look at her. "I didn't want to open that door again.'' It hurt too much, he thought, then realized it still did.

"And saying hello, how's your mama, would have been torture?''

"Yeah, it would have.''

Lisa's lips tightened. Well, that said a lot, she thought.

"Why didn't you come to me?'' he asked.

"I was still married.''

Nash simply stared, wondering if she'd been single would they have gotten back together. And in the same moment he remembered that *she* had dumped *him*.

She'd wanted picket fences and babies, and he couldn't give her that. Aside from the fact that he'd just taken a bullet in the line of duty and lost his partner, he'd watched the devastation hit the widow and cut a strong woman off at the knees. He couldn't do that to Lisa.

The officer returned, interrupting his thoughts and handing him two paper bags. Nash moved back to the table and set them on the floor. He reached into one and pulled out a plastic evidence bag.

"Is this your scarf?"

"Yes." She extended a hand.

He pulled it back. "Evidence."

"What do you mean, evidence? It's my scarf."

"It was found wrapped around the victim's neck, Lisa." Her eyes widened, and she went perfectly still. When she sank back into the chair, he asked, "Now do you want to tell me what you argued about?"

"No, I don't. It was personal."

Nash backed off for now. "Were you angry when you left here?"

"No, I was just tired, Detective."

Nash heard the wall go up between them, even if he couldn't see it. He returned the plastic envelope to the bag. "Do you make teas?"

She blinked, taken aback. "Yes, I do. My herb plants grow quickly in this weather, and I have to cut them back. It's a waste not to do something with the herbs."

"And do you sell the teas at your place of business?"

"Not as a regular commodity, no. I use the cuttings for cooking or rooting new plants. Occasionally I make bath teas, scented bath salts, a couple of mint and catnip drinking teas, and I put them in baskets with a live plant. But it's not a main part of my business, and it's time-consuming to put them together. So I make them up as requested."

"The baskets are for regular sale?"

"No, only with the custom orders. They're handmade, too expensive to make a profit and to keep a reasonable stock of them takes up considerable space." Lisa glanced at the notes he was furiously writing. "Especially because the humidity can rot them. I run a nursery, not a bath-and-tea shop."

"Did you bring one of these custom baskets to the hotel or have it delivered?"

Her brows knitted. "No." Peter would have seen any gift as a peace offering. Heck, she thought, her very presence made him believe she wasn't going to divorce him, although she'd signed the papers weeks before and it had been only a matter of the time line hitting a specified mark. One that had her in deep trouble right now, she suspected.

"Describe the baskets please."

Lisa told him what they looked like, but when she described the brass oval engraved with "Enchanted Garden," he wilted in his chair. She'd bet her best

Kamali pumps that a basket just like one of hers was in that larger bag at his feet.

"Did you speak to anyone on your way to the Baylor Inn, and did anyone see you enter and or exit the building?"

That Nash wouldn't look at her, wouldn't even acknowledge her with so much as a nod as he wrote, made her bristle. "I don't recall. At the time I didn't know I'd need an alibi. Now my husband is dead. My *ex*-husband. And you've all but accused me of his murder."

"I don't have enough evidence for charges."

Something inside her shattered. "We have nothing more to say to each other." She stood. "Unless it's with my lawyer present."

It was on the tip of his tongue to say that, by law, he could hold her for questioning. "I'll need everything you were wearing last night."

"Fine. I'll deliver the clothing to the station within the hour. Are we finished?"

"For now, yes."

Lisa strode to the door. Before she could open it, Nash was there, his hand over her fist.

Her gaze snapped to his. He could taste her fury, it was so pungent.

"Back off, Detective."

He didn't. "Lisa, let's not start like this."

She laughed, sharp and bitter. "We aren't starting a damn thing, Couviyon. We were finished four years ago." *Four years ago when I was pregnant with your child,* she thought, knowing that if she'd ever considered telling him the truth, she sure didn't now.

"You finished it. I didn't."

"You were never *in* the relationship, Nash. You had your own neat version and you kept me on the outside unless we were in bed." She shook off his hand and jerked opened the door.

"Lisa. This is my job."

"I'm thrilled for you. Go do it. And until you have something more than accusations, don't come near me."

She left, striding past the officers. Nash signaled to let her pass. She was pure anger in a snug skirt and high-heeled sandals.

"Seems like a hostile witness, Detective," an officer said.

Nash let out a breath. "Oh, yeah."

Chapter Two

Nash watched Lisa storm off, leaving him feeling twisted and confused. This was why he hadn't dropped by her place to say hello, he thought. She did things to him no other woman had and he still hurt. The humiliation of being dumped by her hardly compared to the feelings of regret he'd had for months after learning she was six hundred miles away walking down the aisle with another man.

Seeing her today warned him he still wasn't over her. Just looking into her eyes stung his heart.

Suddenly Quinn stuck his head out of the room, caught a glimpse of Lisa and whistled softly. Then he looked at Nash.

"That Couviyon charm not working today, laddie?"

Nash eyed Quinn. "You knew she was coming here?"

"I heard the supervisor call her. And yes, I also remembered her married name."

Quinn's look said Nash had had his head in the

sand. Not good for a cop, Nash knew. "She's divorced officially as of this morning."

"So she was still the wife when the victim died?"

Any connection between Lisa and the victim was suspect and damaging, Nash thought. "As I recall, the exact time of death is your job, Kilpatrick," he snarled, pushing past Quinn and into the suite.

Nash ordered a background check on the victim. And his wife.

"Detective?"

Nash rounded, ready to chew someone in two.

A short, wiry man in a black suit stepped into the room. "You couldn't keep this quiet?" he said, glancing around.

Nash's breath snapped out of him. Baylor, the owner of the hotel, and he looked pissed. The day was just getting better and better.

"There are other guests, you know, and they want back into their rooms."

"They will be allowed in soon. And it's a little hard to hide a suspicious death."

The man's eyes were glued to the black body bag rolling away on a stretcher. "Murder?"

Ignoring that, Nash took out his pad, and when he was about to escort Baylor to another room for questioning, the man rushed over to an officer dusting the dresser for prints. "Is that going to leave a stain? This chest is two hundred years old."

The police officer gave Baylor a once-over, then

glanced beyond him to Nash and said, "No sir," before going back to work.

"Sir?" Nash crooked a finger. "You're Mr. Will Baylor?"

The man nodded. "William Reese Baylor IV," he clarified. "I'm the owner. My family built this home over 150 years ago."

"Nice place," Nash said, caring little about Baylor's lineage and the inn's history. His own family had a plantation, Indigo Run, on the edge of town that had been in operation since 1711. "You met the deceased?"

"Briefly when he checked in two days ago. Very nice man. He kept to himself."

"Did he meet anyone here?"

"We don't question our guests so personally. We pride ourselves on privacy, relaxation and discretion."

Nash's gaze narrowed dangerously, and the owner folded.

"Not that I know of. But I'm not here twenty-four seven. With the exception of lunch yesterday, I believe he dined in his suite."

For a man here on business, Winfield didn't do much, Nash thought. Except meet with Lisa. Winfield's PalmPilot indicated he had three meetings but gave no names or times, only dates, and though the victim's laptop was found in the room, they needed a password to access the data.

"How did they get in? Was it someone he knew?" Baylor moved to a set of French doors, but Nash stopped him from opening them, wiggling his own gloved fingers.

"Prints."

Baylor glanced at the officer still kneeling by the chest of drawers. "Oh, yes, of course. This balcony leads to a separate entrance for this room and the one next door. There's a staircase, very narrow and steep, leading to the lower floors outside the kitchen and a path to the patio. It was once the servants' staircase."

The door had an old-fashioned brass latch, one that you had to wrap your hand around to open. With a pen, Nash tried pushing it. It was locked from the inside. But that didn't mean someone couldn't have come up here and left this way. Checking that it had been already dusted, Nash opened it, careful not to step on the porch. Earlier, officers had canvassed the area, and it was going to take some manpower to see if anyone had noticed someone entering the suite through this door. He looked down, then squatted. They hadn't had rain in a while, and the dust level was high. There were several shoe prints in the dust outside the door, and although they'd been lifted and logged already, there were two smaller sets. A woman's?

Nash rubbed his face and straightened. "Who sent the basket?"

The owner frowned and Nash produced the sweet-grass basket with Lisa's logo on the rim.

"I don't know. It's not something we ordered. We provide toiletries for our guests and we have better taste than to offer *homemade* items.'' Baylor made a face at the basket. ''We do seasonal fruit and flavored coffees, too.'' He pointed to the silver tray on a stand near the windows. An officer was collecting it.

Nash stared at the basket. Most of it wasn't home-made, and he wondered again about the teabag-shaped thing dangling from the bathtub faucet.

Another officer stripped the fitted sheet and quilt from the bed.

''No, no, no, that quilt is mine,'' Baylor said.

Nash touched his arm. ''It's evidence. It'll be re-turned to you.''

''It's a hundred years old and in perfect condition, and it had better come back to me that way.'' The odors hit Baylor and he blanched a bit. Death hung in the air like a vapor.

''If it's so precious, why is it displayed on a bed?''

Baylor sniffed. ''Ambiance.''

Nash suppressed the urge to roll his eyes. ''Take that up with forensics.'' He handed him a card.

Baylor snatched it as if snatching the quilt, then looked around at his eighteenth-century-decorated suite. Nash saw him droop with disappointment.

''I'm not going to be able to rent this room for a while,'' he said disparagingly.

''We'll let you know when we're done with it.''

''That's not what I mean. Who'd want to stay here?''

''People die every day.''

Boarding-school posture gripped Baylor's spine. "Not in my inn."

Death was tough for most people. For Nash, it was his career. He spoke for the dead, investigated for them. And he had compassion for the people left behind. But Baylor was more concerned with hotel profits than the fact of a guest's death. Takes all kinds, Nash thought.

"I need a list of who had access to this room. Everyone who has a master key to both doors and who was on duty for the past week."

Baylor nodded.

Nash stared. "Today."

Baylor's expression held more than one man's share of exasperation.

Nash added to it. "I'd like to speak to the staff, too."

"Now? They're busy with guests."

Nash kept writing in his notepad, not looking up. "You know, Mr. Baylor, I'm getting the sense that you don't want us to find out what happened."

"Of course I do. It could have been an accident— maybe he banged his head in the tub or something."

Nash's brows drew together. How did this man know the victim was found wearing only a towel and the bathtub was full of water? Or was he just worried that if that was the case, the family would sue? "Where were you between 5:00 p.m. yesterday and this morning, Mr. Baylor?"

If the victim had been dead nine hours, then Nash had to narrow the suspect list.

Baylor gave Nash a look that said he thought himself beyond reproach. "I'll give you my schedule. Follow me, and I'll introduce you to the concierge."

THE CONCIERGE, John Chartres, was a tall, narrow man with equally confined features, and for someone living in a southern seaboard town, he was as pale as the white shirt beneath his tailored suit. His black hair was swept back with a severity that sharpened his face and made his eyes and lips look vibrant against his skin. He wore disdain like a tie, and he rose from behind the delicate desk like a king from his throne. *Oh, yeah, that says welcome to the Baylor real well,* Nash thought cynically.

Then the man spoke and the New York accent, however he tried to hide it, hurt Nash's ears.

"I didn't see anyone go to his suite specifically. Perhaps you should question the housekeeping staff. I'm usually in my office."

"Isn't it your job to know all the guests? To see that their stay is perfect?"

"I delegate well."

I'll bet. And actually working your job was for the little people, Nash thought. "Did you know Mr. Winfield?"

"Other than his face and name, no. He was only a guest."

Nash kept his features relaxed, but that the man kept

shuffling through papers and not looking him in the eye said he was hiding something. Nash would have to dig a little with this one.

"You have a key to the door to the back staircase?"

"I have a key to every door in this hotel."

"I'll need a list of which keys each employee carries and where they are kept."

Chartres gestured and Nash followed the man into the reception area and behind the counter.

Nash's gaze swept the rows of keys. "You're kidding, right? Anyone could take these." The keys weren't the computer-card type but old-fashioned brass, which he was sure added the same sort of ambiance as the antique quilt.

"Each room has inside locks, as well, and though they look old, they aren't." Chartres handed a key over.

It was chiseled like a house key, but the tab was brass with Victorian scroll.

"The balcony doors have no outside handles," Chartres said, then explained, "The staff doesn't use it. Though it's sturdy, in keeping with the historical accuracy, the staircase remains steep and narrow. We discourage guests from opening the doors unless they are in residence. There is a push latch in case the door closes, but the inside lock must be disengaged."

So, Nash thought, if anyone came into the room from that direction, the guest had to be expecting them and the locks had to be disengaged. The balcony doors had been locked from the inside when the police had arrived. Had Winfield opened them for his killer? Or his ex-wife? Even as the thought careened through his head, Nash hated himself for it. Lisa was not capable of murder. Not the Lisa he once knew.

"You said you were on duty?" Nash asked.

"Yes. And if you don't mind, can we take this back into my office?"

As they headed in that direction, Chartres lagged behind, smiling at an elderly couple approaching the reception area. He slipped behind the gleaming counter to retrieve a few slips of paper, handing them to the couple. "Your phone messages," Chartres said to them. "And your 7:00 p.m. reservations at Emily's are set."

Nash had to admit that when Chartres was talking with the hotel patrons, he was all smiles and warmth. The couple inquired about the police cars and ambulance, and Chartres explained that a guest had passed away during the night and for them not to worry. But then Nash shouldered his way past, introduced himself and questioned the elderly couple. It gained him nothing. Though their rooms were on the floor below, they insisted they were sound sleepers.

Chartres gestured to the office. "That was rude, Detective."

"A policeman's job is often rude. Everyone is a potential witness." Nash's look said the concierge was on that list, and Chartres stiffened, affronted. "At what time did you leave your post?" Nash asked once they were in the small office.

"I didn't."

"Not to eat, not to use the bathroom?"

"No. Meals are brought here, if I want. And I didn't."

"You didn't make the rounds during the cocktail and dinner hour?"

"No."

Then who's to say he was even in the office? Nash thought. "You have a popular restaurant in this hotel, Mr. Chartres. You didn't leave your office and stroll through, introducing yourself?"

"It was a quiet night."

"Quiet enough not to notice someone heading up to Mr. Winfield's room?"

"Apparently. This hotel is more like a home, the atmosphere unobstructed. It's why we do so well. Not all the suites are occupied, anyway. We don't check on the comings and goings of guests, only that while they're here, they're happy."

"You had a delivery to a room, yet no one seems to recall receiving it."

"What delivery?

"A basket from Enchanted Garden."

"It may have been a gift from someone. All deliveries are signed for and recorded." Chartres swiveled his chair toward a computer screen and tapped the keys. He peered. "The only deliveries were the daily flowers for the rooms, a guest's dry cleaning and a package from High Cotton for the elderly couple you saw, which was placed in their room."

That high-school class in shorthand came in handy sometimes, Nash thought as Chartres tried to sneak peeks at his notes. After a few more questions, Chartres printed out a list of the staff and phone numbers and a schedule roster. Nash folded it into his leather notebook, then stood, offering his hand. Chartres's palm was smooth and dry, his grip firm.

Nash left, heading back upstairs again to check the outer doors. Officers were almost finished with the room and had double-checked outside for footprints. Nash opened the door and studied the deck, the path down to the first and second floors. He wondered if Baylor had the floor plans to this place and walked across the balcony and down the stairs. A private home was tucked only yards away, beside the hotel, and a privacy fence carved a smart line between the properties. The inn dining room was to the rear, a sizable portion of seating outdoors on a stone patio surrounded by exotic flowering shrubs and shaded with umbrellas. It was empty now.

Nash climbed back up the stairs to look around the suite once more. Was the scarf the murder weapon? If not, Winfield could have died from anything, food poisoning or heart trouble. Until he had an autopsy, Nash was finished here. He'd collect reports from the other officers, run a check on Winfield, and then he'd know where to go from there. At the moment there was too little evidence to point him in any direction.

Except at Lisa.

He was done for now, anyway, he reasoned and

returned to his office, dropping into his chair and tossing his notebook on the desk. He dug the heels of his palms into his eyes, then sagged back into the chair. A bag of clothing marked "Lisa Bracket Winfield" was sealed and on his desk. A note from the sheriff said she'd offered prints before they'd asked. Her angry expression flashed like lightning in his mind. He could have handled that confrontation better, he thought. He knew he hadn't accused her of the crime, but the questions always made people defensive. But what the hell was she hiding?

Winfield had been pushed to his death, but his instincts told Nash there was more than a silk scarf connecting this to Lisa. And he never ignored his instincts.

The phone shrilled and before it reached a second ring he snatched it up. "Couviyon."

"Detective, this is Kathy Boon. I'm a housekeeper at the Baylor Inn. They, I mean my boss, wanted me to call you to tell you that I saw a woman go into Mr. Winfield's room."

"Describe her please."

"Red hair, long, in a ponytail tied with a scarf. Killer outfit. Lime-green skirt, same color top but it had polka dots on it. She was about five-eight, I'd guess. Pretty. I noticed her because her handbag and shoes matched her skirt and not too many people can get away with wearing that color."

Nash allowed himself a smile, then glanced at the shopping bag of clothes Lisa had turned in. "What time was it when you saw this woman?"

"About eight-thirtyish, maybe quarter to nine. I work till midnight, then come in at five, so that's why I wasn't around this morning."

"Did you see her leave?"

"No, I didn't, but that doesn't mean anything. I go from the laundry to the rooms about a dozen times a night."

"Did you see anyone else enter Mr. Winfield's room?"

"Room service at about six."

Winfield had been alive at six. The attendant had already confirmed delivering the meal around then. "Did you hear anything coming from Mr. Winfield's room?"

She was quiet.

"Ma'am?"

"I'm thinking. No...well, I'm not sure. I heard arguing at a little past nine, but not enough to call the cops or anything. Oh, God, maybe I should have."

"You couldn't have known, ma'am."

As she spoke, Nash checked the employee roster and found her name, marking beside it. His head was swimming, mostly with images of Lisa and the absolute fury she'd thrown at him.

"If I have any more questions, I'll call you."

"Yeah, sure, and if I think of anything more, I'll let you know."

He hung up and leaned back in his chair. Lisa had definitely been there. He hoped the coroner came back with something soon. Lisa wasn't capable of hurting anyone. At least not physically. And as he remembered their conversation, he recognized his own bitterness, as well as hers.

What would have happened, he wondered, if he'd fought for her all those years ago? If he'd gone to her and said...what? That he loved her? Unfortunately he hadn't realized he loved her until she was walking down the aisle with someone else and he was miles away regretting it.

The phone shrilled, jerking him from unhappy musing. He grabbed the receiver and punched line one. "Detective Couviyon."

"Hey, Nash, this is your favorite lab rat."

Nash smiled. The coroner, Quinn Kilpatrick. "Tell me you have something for me, good buddy."

"The deceased died between ten and midnight. I'll have more specific analysis in a few hours, a day max."

"Cause of death?"

"Toxic poisoning."

"What about the scarf?"

"That was after the fact. Poisoning looks like an overdose of digitalis, near as I can tell, but if you quote me right now, I'll deny it."

"How did he get it?"

"An injection, in a drink, food—a number of ways."

"Could he have overdosed accidentally?"

"I don't know. It's hard to nail this element, and

I'm waiting on his med records to see if he was being treated for anything. Be patient.''

Nash didn't have any patience today and struggled for a scrap. "I thought you couldn't detect digitalis."

"That's why you can't quote me."

Nash hung up and studied his notes. Winfield had lived in New York and the NYPD had been notified. The victim's apartment would be sealed off and swept for evidence. It was time, he thought, to find more suspects. Yet in the back of his mind lingered one troubling question. Had Lisa Bracket Winfield changed enough over the past four years to be capable of murder?

LISA SLID INTO the booth in the diner and smiled at her lawyer, Trisha Flynn. Trish had her notebook out, ready to talk.

"We could have met at the office, Lisa."

Lisa shook her head, grateful for the cup of coffee waiting for her. "That would make me feel like a real suspect."

"From what you told me, you're the best possible one."

"Gosh, you're a fun date, huh?" Lisa's heart sank and at the same time, anger unfolded. Was Peter going to keep ruining her life? "Dammit, Trish, I didn't do this," she said, trying to keep her voice down. "When I left Peter last night, he was very much alive."

"And mad as hell, I'll bet."

Lisa scoffed. "He wasn't getting his way, so yes,

he was mad." Lisa glanced at the menu, and they ordered, silent till the waitress left them.

"Was it the same argument?" Trish asked.

"Oh, yes. When was it not?"

"You don't look upset that he's dead."

"I grieved. I loved him once upon a time." *And I loved Nash, too,* she thought, and knew if it had been him who died, she wouldn't be functioning nearly as well. "But you know better than anyone what it was like with him, Trish. And now to have Nash nosing around in my personal business, my marriage..."

"You should have told him."

Trisha had been with her when she'd miscarried her baby. "Is that my lawyer or friend talking?" Lisa asked.

Trisha smiled, her dark hair sweeping over her shoulder as she reached for the creamer. "Your friend. Who's on lawyer time."

Lisa tried to smile and couldn't. "I know you think Nash should know about the baby I lost, but I understand him better than he does. It wouldn't have worked out then, and bringing it up now will only hurt him more." Four years had eased the loss only a little.

"But Nash wants to know what you and Peter fought about."

"I can't, Trish." Lisa's eyes teared up, and she grabbed a paper napkin, blotting them. *Wimp,* she thought, *you've been through worse.* "I'm sorry."

"It's okay, honey. We've all been there." Lisa met

her gaze. "Do you want me to petition to have him removed from the case?"

"You can do that?"

"He has a personal attachment."

"No, it will just make me look guilty."

"Is Nash an honest man, Lisa?" her lawyer asked. She didn't hesitate. "Yes."

"Would he use this to hurt you?"

"I...I don't think so."

Trish voiced no opinion on that, and Lisa wondered how bad this was going to get. "Okay, the conversation you and Peter had last night is inadmissible, and your word against a dead man's is hearsay," Trisha said. "Don't worry about it now. It has no bearing on his death that I can see."

Lisa relaxed back into the leather seat and nursed her coffee. "And if Nash believes it does?"

"Let's wait to see what they come up with, because right now, we know you didn't kill Peter."

Lisa was grateful Trisha believed her, but the certainty that Nash didn't was brewing like a storm inside her.

"Do you want me to hire a private detective to find out what I can?"

"No."

Trisha eyed her, making notes.

"The police are working on it, Trish. I'm innocent."

"Nash has already ordered a deep background check on Peter and it will include you."

Lisa shrugged. "That can't be helped."

"And if he reads medical records?"

Suddenly Lisa went still. "Don't they have to get a court order?"

"Not if you're a suspect. And if you want to look innocent, you give them permission."

"I'll cross that bridge when I have to." But the thought of telling Nash the truth gave her nothing but pain. He might still be a little hurt, but the truth would destroy him.

Their food arrived. Lisa stared down at the healthy-looking green salad, then called the waitress back.

"I'll start with dessert. Chocolate. Anything with chocolate."

"Woman after my own heart," the waitress said as she left.

Trisha shook her head, smiling.

Lisa shrugged. "Hey, I'll jog an extra two miles."

A minute later the waitress slid the dessert before her. And both women gaped at the five-layer torte covered in chocolate fudge.

"Better make that five miles," Trisha said, laughing. "With sit-ups."

Lisa stabbed a chunk of torte enjoying the calories one at a time. "You could join me, but I know how you look running in those high heels you refuse to lose. It ain't pretty, sugah."

Trisha smiled and forked a bite of the dessert.

Lisa devoured bite after bite, knowing that not even gooey chocolate would keep her mind off Nash and that he thought she was capable of murder.

Chapter Three

The next day Lisa was still fuming, and the best thing for her temper was to dig in the dirt. Leaving Kate to oversee the register, she repotted new stock and replaced the plants in the smaller gardens that had been sold in the past few days. She scrubbed terra-cotta pots, clipped cuttings, clipped herbs and tied them to dry, then deadheaded flowers. Anything to keep her mind off Nash Couviyon and the fact that he thought she was capable of killing another human being. It made her ill. And it hurt.

Lord, it hurt.

Obviously whatever relationship they'd had—and she still wasn't certain they'd had a real one—meant nothing. Not when you're faced with murder charges, she supposed.

Peter was dead. She grieved for him of course, but it was mild. That shamed her. She'd been his wife, in name only for the past three years. Still. He didn't deserve to die, although she'd learned quickly in their marriage that he wasn't a very nice person. Once she wore his ring, he'd become controlling, manipulative, obsessive.

He'd damn near driven her crazy in a few short months. And she'd learned her true purpose in his life. Be pretty, behave, give great parties, and schmooze…

A trophy wife.

Boy, did he learn he'd chosen poorly. And so did she. She'd left and started over. Started over a couple of times, in fact, she mused, and now she had every cent she'd earned in the past three years sunk into this house and her nursery business. She'd done most of the work herself and business was steady. Temple Couviyon had steered some contractors her way for her more exotic plants. Life was getting back to good, she thought, and felt as if she'd spent a century getting to this very moment.

And now it could be over. If word leaked out that she was a suspect in a murder case, she'd be ruined. Her reputation would be shot.

Shaking her head, she plowed her hands deep into the potting soil she was mixing. Though the fresh compost smelled fine, the stench of cow manure was strong enough to make her eyes water.

It was how Nash found her. Elbow deep in black dirt, pausing to add vermiculite to the mix. Outside the greenhouse, she kneaded and folded the soil, and although there were tears in her eyes, her expression said she wasn't crying. She looked on that road between pissed off and pleased.

Nash wasn't sure he should interrupt. "Lisa?"

She hesitated, then kept folding dirt in the large galvanized tub.

"What is it, Detective?" Lisa recognized his voice instantly, almost felt his presence before he spoke. It was irritating as hell that he could still do that to her.

He moved to her side. She glanced at him.

The impact of those green eyes left him momentarily hurting for air. "Peter was poisoned."

Her head whipped to the side, her eyes wide. "Good Lord, how?"

"That we don't know yet. Did he have heart trouble?"

She snorted and went back to mixing. "No. He was never sick. He's...he was a guru about eating healthy foods, taking vitamins. Working out. It was really annoying that the man wouldn't relax and just have fun. Be a slug, lie like a potato." She bit her lip, knowing she'd said more than she should have. "I don't think I should talk to you without a lawyer present."

"You haven't been charged."

"And that makes a difference?"

"Cooperating will go in your favor. Do you want to impede an investigation?"

"I've told you all I can recall."

"Except what you and Peter discussed, exactly."

"He wanted me back... It doesn't matter," she said tiredly. "He was alive when I left him." She moved to the sink and washed her hands. "I get it. You don't have motive."

"You were his wife—"

"Ex, or soon to be, at the time," she stressed.

"—and you stood to gain. On the day of his death you were still legally married."

"Splitting hairs, Nash. I didn't ask for anything of his when I left him, and I hadn't been his wife in any sense, including the biblical, for three years."

Nash's brows shot up. Where had she been all this time? "Not according to the legal system."

"Fine. Have it your way. You always do."

"What's that supposed to mean?"

She turned, resting her rear against the sink edge and drying her hands. For a second she debated opening up this can of worms, then decided he could take a piece of the truth. "Four years ago you wanted me to wait around till you were ready for more than a few dates a month."

Nash said nothing, bracing for the attack.

"You wanted me to be yours, but you weren't willing to ever claim me. Even your brothers thought I was just a *friend*."

The bitterness in her voice smacked him across the face. They'd shared a bed, shared each other, dammit. "So you went elsewhere?"

"I was still here before I met Peter and a couple of months after that." She hooked the towel on a peg near the sink. "It doesn't matter that it didn't work out. At least I did something about it. Fish or cut bait, you know."

"You'd have wanted to force me into something I didn't want, then?"

She made a face. "No. Which is why I ended it."
So he wouldn't feel he had to do the right thing because of their baby, she thought. "But that's not the point. Face it, Nash. You weren't ready for me."

"You didn't give me a chance."

She made a sound between a laugh and disgust. "You had plenty of chances. You just didn't want me the way I wanted you." *Forever.*

There was hurt in her voice, a hint of it, barely disguised. She pushed past him, but didn't make it far.

He caught her arm, the move putting her nearly against him. "My God, Lisa, did you think I didn't care about you?" His gaze raked her face as he searched for something to grasp and knew he shouldn't even be trying.

"Caring was all I got from you." *And a baby I never got to hold,* she thought.

Nash struggled with his heart. He wanted to say things, things she needed to hear and he wanted to tell. But he couldn't. Not when just looking at her pushed the heat simmering between them up a notch. Even in the apron and grubby T-shirt and steaming mad, she turned him inside out. He'd always felt incredible heat and electricity with her, more than anyone else. He'd never trusted it. And there was more here, this time. Yet the expression on her face said he didn't have a chance. And the fact that he was prying into her life and considered her a prime suspect wasn't helping his position. Did he want something with her? Was he willing to resurrect the past? No. Attraction

was only about hormones, he thought, and forced himself to shut off the thoughts and turn up his cop brain.

He let her go. After a moment he asked, "What
herbs and flowers do you use to make the teas?"

Back to detecting, she thought, rubbing the warmth
from her arm. "For the bath I use lavender, rosemary,
lemon balm…eucalyptus, if I have it. For drinking…mint, lemon mint, chamomile and catnip. A couple of other herbs if they're growing well." Her frown
deepened. "Why?"

"I'm not at liberty to say right now." Because he
wasn't certain how the digitalis got into Winfield's
system.

"Fine. Didn't I tell you to talk to my lawyer next
time you wanted to ask me anything?"

Nash pushed his fingers through his hair. "What are
you hiding?"

"Not a thing."

"Then talk to me."

"Considering we have a past, I don't think that's
wise."

He knew she was right. It was almost a matter of
pride to be objective with her stomping on his every
effort. "I'm not trying to send you to jail over four-
year-old jilted feelings, for pity's sake."

"Jilted, Nash? You have to be engaged to be
jilted."

With that she marched up the steps and into the
house.

NASH SPENT the rest of the day trying not to brood and went through Winfield's briefcase again. For a broker, there wasn't much there. It was as if he'd put together this briefcase for just this trip. The PalmPilot gave Winfield's schedule in New York, yet the appointments stopped the day he flew into nearby Charleston. There was a notation of a number. Nash called it. He got the Baylor Inn. Okay, nothing new there. What about the blank real-estate contracts in the victim's briefcase?

He backtracked and called the man's lawyer. After a ten-minute conversation in which Nash explained that his client was dead and privacy would only hinder finding out who killed him, the lawyer told him that Winfield had gone to Indigo to take up with old acquaintances and perhaps purchase property. No, the attorney said, he didn't know what property Winfield was interested in. The record of Winfield's calls from the hotel produced only one—to Lisa.

Nash spent the remainder of the afternoon calling Realtors and came up empty. Winfield hadn't contacted any of the Indigo Realtors, but that didn't mean he wasn't searching outside the area. Maybe Winfield had been looking at real estate in Charleston, and was just using Indigo as a base because Lisa was here. Nash would have to widen his search and wondered what unsuspecting rookie he could sic on the job. Maybe Winfield spoke directly with the property owners?

Nash stared at the pile of evidence he still had.

Blank sale contracts. A PalmPilot that held nothing past the day he'd arrived and a laptop with a password even his best tech experts couldn't get around. Then there was the picture of Lisa.

Talk to me, Winfield. Who wanted you dead?

He reached for the phone to call New York and see what the police had found in Winfield's apartment, but caught a glance at the time. He muttered a curse and quit for the day, but when he was driving home, he decided to swing by the Baylor Inn and see if he could learn how the gift basket got into the hotel room. Although the concierge said all deliveries were recorded and signed for, the gift basket got past the reception desk somehow. This time, Nash went to talk to the lowest man on the totem pole. And struck gold.

The bellman, Mick, a young blond about eighteen, gave him an exasperated look. He was on his break and didn't want to spend it talking to the police. "Look, man, I don't know what else to tell you. It was the messenger service half the town uses. Mercury."

Nash was relieved. Lisa had said she hadn't delivered a basket. "Did you check it, stop them?"

"No. Not only is it not my job, they come in all the time—messages, flowers, deliveries from local shops. People vacation here, y'know, they buy stuff and don't want to carry it around, so they have it delivered. The delivery people just go right to the room if they know which one. If no one's there to accept it, they drop it off at the desk and I take it up later. I didn't. Not to Mr. Winfield.''

This wasn't the efficient picture the concierge had painted. "So you remember Winfield?''

The teen snorted. "Yeah, I do. He was a good tipper, but the man wanted you to practically cough up a lung for him for the cash.''

Nash smirked, wondering how Lisa could marry a guy like that. "Can you describe the messenger?''

"My height, black hair. Wearing a helmet, goggles and bike shorts.''

Nash had seen the riders around and made a note to call Mercury Messenger Service. At least he was getting somewhere. The searches on the other employees' pasts would take a bit to compile. And read.

"What time was it when you saw the delivery?''

"About six.''

Nash dismissed the kid after handing him his card and reminding him that if he recalled anything else to phone him. The teen slouched away and Nash set out to find Kathy Boon; he was lucky enough to find her just starting her shift. She was in a second-floor storage room tying her sneakers.

She smiled brightly and the smile stayed there when he flashed his badge. "You caught me at a good time—I just got here.''

She was younger than he'd expected and she sure as hell didn't look like a housekeeper. Peaches-and-cream skin was the first thing he noticed, then her eyes, crystal-blue and set gently in an angelic face.

Rich, nut-colored hair surrounded her face and spilled onto her shoulders in fat curls. And man, did she have curves. Compact and wearing shorts and a polo shirt bearing the inn's logo, she was adorable.

"Come on," she said, curling a rubber band around the ponytail of hair. Still smiling, she inclined her head as she pushed a cart that looked too heavy for her to manage down the hall. "I didn't think of anything else, Detective Couviyon."

"It's pronounced coo-vee-yon," he corrected, smiling back. "Do you recall a messenger coming to Winfield's room?"

She knocked on a suite door, called out, then let herself in with her passkey. "No, sorry. I didn't see anyone but the redhead in lime-green. You should sit down, darlin'. You look exhausted."

He was, and couldn't recall the last time he ate, but continued, "Have you ever used the back stairs?"

"Good grief, no. Too steep and I don't trust them. Plus, there's no reason to trek up there." She collected used glasses and plates, depositing them outside the door.

"Have you ever seen anyone go up there?"

"To the balcony? Only the guests use the balcony to watch the sunset. It's eye-popping gorgeous, but I bet from up there, it's magnificent."

"Are you from around here?"

She kept her head down as she polished an antique clothes press. "No, farther north. Is there anything else, Detective? I've got six suites to clean and a double shift.''

Nash heard the sudden chill in her tone and frowned.

''Miss Boon?''

She looked up, her expression blank as a card.

''Is there something you'd like to tell me?''

She looked thoughtful and he wondered if his suspicion was valid. ''No, I don't think so.''

Her hand trembled a bit as she lifted a vase and dusted beneath it. Nash recognized fear. Of him or of something else? ''If you do think of anything else, call me.''

She nodded mutely. He slipped out of the room and didn't see her drop to the bed and cover her face with her hands.

THE NEXT MORNING, after leftover Chinese food and a lousy night's sleep, Nash nursed a cup of double-shot cappuccino from the Daily Grind while he waited for Kilpatrick to show up. The coroner's office wasn't exactly his favorite spot to spend the morning, but a vague message from Quinn had gotten him there early.

''It's a bold and brash lad who thinks he can put his feet on my desk.''

Nash slid his feet to the floor and smiled. ''I've never been known for subtlety. Didn't think you were so possessive.''

''Never assume, Couviyon,'' Quinn said.

''So what did you find?'' Nash asked.

Quinn looked insulted. "What? No 'thank you, Quinn, for the extra hours and being brilliant? For breaking a date with the cutest creature to walk in this town in six months?'"

"Oh, yeah, who?"

"Kate Holling. Lisa's employee."

Nash frowned. He didn't remember the woman beyond blond hair and gold lipstick with dark liner. Kate didn't seem like Quinn's type. He usually went for the more exotic. "So was it worth the overtime?" He gestured to the lab.

Quinn flicked on all the lights and Nash winced at the fluorescent glare as the man moved to the coffee-maker and started a pot. "You could have been gracious and done this, you know."

"With all these chemicals? I'd kill us."

Quinn flipped the switch and faced him. "I found the exact cause and the method."

"No kidding?"

Quinn slid a faintly insulted look to Nash, then said, "It wasn't digitalis."

"Good thing I didn't quote you, then."

"It was similar enough to be mistaken for causing heart failure, though."

Impatient for coffee, Quinn pulled the pot out, shoved a cup under the drip, then reversed them. He sipped, making a face. "Field rations," he murmured.

Quinn inclined his head, and the pair moved to the computer at the rear of the lab. The coroner tapped a few keys, calling up the results, and as they flicked and spread on the screen, he slipped into his lab coat.

"You owe my assistant Jarred for this. He's the one who did a baseline for flowers."

Flowers. Nash felt his heart slowly sinking to his stomach. Resigned, he settled into the neighboring chair and listened.

"The poison wasn't ingested and here's your murder weapon." He dropped the evidence bag on the table in front of Nash.

Nash simply stared, feeling any hope drain away like rain down a gutter. It was the bath tea.

"That teabag in the hot water released the flower and herbal properties. Mostly the essential oils. Good for mood therapy and fragrance."

"What was in it?"

"Lavender, rosemary." Quinn met his gaze and added proudly, "Lily of the valley."

"And?" Nash made a rolling motion for more.

"*Convallaria majalis,* better known as lily of the valley, is highly toxic, especially the leaves. Steeping it released the oils from the leaves, which are more toxic than the petals. The poison is a glycoside called convallatoxin, which works similarly to digitalis."

"So you weren't far off."

Quinn snorted. Nash knew that wasn't good enough for Quinn, in or out of the lab.

"All it has to do is seep into an orifice or a wound, and it starts working. Winfield had a couple of cuts on his back that look like scratches to me." Quinn showed him pictures, pointing. "Other than that, the man had skin like a baby. If he dunked under the steaming water, got even a fraction of oil in his nose or mouth, he was as good as dead if he didn't get help immediately."

"Judging by the burned-down candles, I'd say he soaked for a while."

"Didn't have to," Quinn said. "This works fast, and although dosage would be hard to judge, there was enough in that bath tea to kill him. He'd have felt too warm first, a headache, tense, instead of feeling relaxed. I imagine he stayed in the bath for a while, hoping that would go away, but in doing so, he just made it worse by giving the toxin more opportunity to get inside him." Quinn tapped a spot on the pictures of Winfield's body. "Remember the red patches? That's part of the reaction, then hallucinations. He had dilated pupils, excess salivation—proved from the residue and stains—and then pop, heart failure."

"How long did it take?"

Quinn hit print on the computer. "From the exact time of death, I'd say an hour, maybe less."

"God."

"His heart wouldn't have seized, but just slowed to a stop. He would've been too weak to talk. Then to even breathe."

Quinn leaned back in his chair, fingers wrapped around his mug. "The teabag did him in." He stared into his mug, his voice soft, his lilt deeper. "I've seen men go down before with some hellacious wounds, but never for taking a bath.'' Quinn met his gaze. ''Whoever did this knew about toxins.''

''And knew Winfield would use the teabag.''

''Oh, yeah, just not when. So timing would have been everything. The killer could have left this, counting on him to use it that evening, and then left him to die while he created a great alibi. This stuff works fast.'' Quinn sipped. ''Poor man was done before he hit the bed.''

Nash cursed.

Quinn's gaze speared him over the rim of the mug. ''And here I thought you'd be warm and fuzzy all over, Couviyon,'' he said dryly.

Lisa didn't have an alibi. ''Just how common is lily of the valley?''

''The flower? Fairly.'' Quinn leaned back in his chair, straining to reach a case of books. He slid his fingers over the spines, then plucked one out. He thumbed, spread the pages and handed it to Nash.

He stared at the picture. ''I see this all the time.''

''Now ask me how many people would know what it can do.'' He held up a finger for a second. ''Personal opinion, not professional. I would never stake my rep on statistics.''

Nash arched a brow.

''I'd say one out of seventy would know what it can do. Some would know it was poisonous, like most mothers of small children, and florists, horticulturists. Gardeners.''

Nash's expression fell further.

"Your prime suspect is Lisa, isn't it?' Quinn's voice was soft.

"Yes."

Quinn collected the report and slid it into a clean folder. "I don't believe it." He held out the report.

Nash took it, fingering the edges. "Me neither, but the evidence against her is stacking up."

"It's too obvious."

Nash's gaze shot to Quinn's.

"She's a gardener, horticulturist and the victim's ex-wife. If she wanted to kill the man, then she went about it the wrong way. And she's not stupid."

"I've considered a setup," Nash said, insulted.

"All right, so where's your motive? She left him quite a while ago, wanted to cut the ties enough to not take anything from him."

"How do you know all this?"

"Bought some plants from her a couple of months ago and I took her out for lunch. Great lady. Dynamite legs. Wish she'd have fallen all over me, but…"

Nash's expression shifted from surprise to anger in a matter of seconds.

"I didn't tell you because it never really came up. Besides, you two had only dated four years ago. Nothing serious."

Well, if that isn't the kick in the pants, Nash thought as Quinn stood and went back to the coffeemaker to pour himself a fresh, less-lethal cup.

"Yeah, right." Nash stood, gripping the report, and walked to the door.

"She's gotten to you again, eh, lad?"

"Shut up, Kilpatrick."

Quinn laughed, a deep, rich and damn annoying sound that followed Nash out to his car.

On the way into his office, Nash's cell phone rang. He flipped it open.

"Detective Rhinehart, NYPD," said his caller. "Winfield's lawyer said the man was insured out the ass."

Nash frowned. "How much?"

"Two million."

"Was he worth that much?"

"Not a chance. His wife, Lisa, is the sole beneficiary, too."

Nash felt ice drip down his spine. "But she's divorced from him."

"Yes, now. But she was married to him when he died."

Nash scrambled for a theory to dispute that. "That's a matter of hours, and according to the coroner, the poison took at least an hour. That's pretty sketchy timing if she wanted to be married at the time of death so she'd get his death benefit."

"As long as it was before midnight. And married or not, I believe she gets the booty."

"I don't buy it."

"Got anything else?"

"Not yet."

Nash questioned the man further, asked for a copy

of the policy, then hung up. His chest felt suddenly too tight for his lungs. Damn.

Now he had motive, method and opportunity.

He was angry enough to spit nails, but he didn't want his emotions to get in the way. The motive was thin, as was the timing of the toxin. Lisa had left the hotel by nine-thirty. Quinn said the victim died between eleven-thirty and midnight. If it took an hour for the toxin to bring Winfield to death, then he had to have used the bath tea after Lisa left. But had it been in the room all the time, before she arrived, and she just didn't see it? And if the divorce left Lisa without a cent, was this a way to finally make him pay?

Two million reasons were hard to ignore.

Chapter Four

The next evening, Nash approached Lisa's house,
dread running down his spine in slow rivers. He knew
he was breaking the rules about getting personally involved with a suspect, but reasoned that he did have
to question her. *Man, that's weak,* he thought, and the
fact that she'd refused to speak with him about anything without her lawyer got pushed to the wayside.
Besides, her lawyer, Trisha Flynn, was aware of the
two-million-dollar policy that just recently made Lisa
a rich woman. Winfield's attorney had called Flynn.
Nash had been on the phone with the woman half the
afternoon. Flynn argued that Lisa was not aware of the
policy. Nash had to be sure.

He stopped on the porch and rang the bell. The light
above his head glowed bug-burner yellow, and like
comforting arms closing around him, jasmine made a
slow crawl over the white-railed porch. The fragrance
was faintly sweet, the vines falling around potted
plants and wicker furniture. With his brother Temple
being a landscaper, he recognized begonias blooming

alongside casual mums, partnered with willowy calla lilies and fat gerbera daisies. As porches went, Lisa's was homey and welcoming, and so was her low-country-style bungalow. He couldn't help but wonder if things had turned out differently, would they have had a place like this?

He didn't have time to think more on that before soft footsteps sounded from inside, and when she flung the door open, he was surprised to see she was crying.

Lisa groaned and snapped, "What do you want?" She dashed at her wet cheeks with the back of her hand.

"What's wrong?" He stepped closer and instinctively glanced past her into the house. "Are you okay?"

"Oh, gee, I'm a murder suspect, my ex-husband is dead, and my former boyfriend is trying to send me to jail. What do you think, Detective?"

He met her gaze, then pulled a handkerchief from his back pocket and handed it to her. "I'm trying to keep you out of jail. I know it's rough, Lisa."

His tender tone sank into her like a hot little arrow. "Like you're making it any easier?" Lisa stared at the folded hanky. He'd always had one, neatly folded and ready to offer. It was a gentlemanly gesture, and she'd missed it.

"It's not my job to make it easy. I investigate and gather the facts."

She wiped her eyes and nose, then met his gaze.

"Yeah, well, you're not digging deep enough in my opinion."

"I figured that." He *was* trying, he thought.

"Is this official? Because if it is, I've taken all the copspeak I can for the day."

"Half and half."

She eyed him. "I suppose you want to talk about this insurance policy."

"Yes. If you'd like your lawyer with you, I can wait."

She snickered under her breath. "It would serve you right to come head-to-head with Trisha, but no. Come on in. She told me and I've nothing to hide." Lisa stepped back, her sweeping gesture drawing him inside. She closed the door and flipped on more lights. "Want some decaf coffee? A beer?" She headed deeper into the house.

"Coffee's fine." Nash hadn't expected her to be so amiable, and he felt his guard slip a little. He followed her, his gaze moving over the comfortable traditional decor of the house, then to the woman who owned it. Her red hair spilled to mid-spine and gleamed in the low light. Wearing a snug-fitting rust-colored top and brown Capri pants, she moved around the kitchen, slipping the carafe under the faucet and grabbing a pair of mugs. While coffee brewed, she pulled out a ribbon-tied box and placed cookies onto a plate.

"Have a seat, Nash."

He slid onto a stool. "Your house is great, Lisa."

She paused to glance at him, and Nash felt electrified by the single look. "Thanks. Me and the bank are quite pleased with ourselves."

He smiled and set his notebook on the counter. "Did you do it all yourself?"

"No," she said. "Hoisting the ceiling supports and shingling the roof were a little out of my skill range."

"Very funny."

She turned and placed the plate on the counter. "I try." She added cream and sugar containers, then hunted down spoons. "The house is fairly new, but the design is old."

"You sure snap out of a bad mood quickly, but then, you always did."

Lisa didn't want to be reminded of how it had been between them. It had been good, but not going anywhere. And would have ended faster than it had if he'd known she had been pregnant with his child. "I wasn't in a bad mood, just feeling sorry for myself."

"Why?"

"Other than the obvious, I got a call from the funeral home in New York and Peter's lawyers. He didn't have any family left, so I guess I'm the closest thing to that. Anyway, I asked if they'd like me to come to New York to make the burial arrangements, and the director said it wasn't necessary." She stilled, then shook her head and filled two mugs. "Peter had made the arrangements down to the last detail. Even the flowers, where they're to be placed, the music." She turned from the window counter and faced the island, sliding a mug in front of him. "I know it's a wise thing to do, but it all seems so calculated."

"Its not a time that people want to make decisions like that." And why had Winfield done all this at such a young age? Was he expecting an enemy to take him out?

She lifted her gaze and said quietly, "He had one for me, too, Nash. I didn't even know this. He didn't consult me, and according to the funeral director, he even had the dress I'm to be buried in already stored."

Nash's brows rose. "Okay, that's to the right of creepy."

"Isn't it? And our plots are in the same spot, one on top of the other."

"Eternally yours, huh?"

Suddenly she covered her heart, her eyes wide. "He used to say that. All the time."

"I'm sorry."

She waved dismissively. "No, don't be, but it just makes me angrier that he did this behind my back." She took a sip of her drink, then grabbed the plate. "Let's go in the living room where it's more comfortable."

Nash nodded, grabbed his notebook and followed her. Placing the plate on the coffee table, she settled into a corner of the sofa. He sat down on the other end, but instantly knew it was a mistake. Her perfume, a light scent of jasmine, reached out its tendrils and wrapped around him. Suddenly he recalled all he'd shut out of his mind—the taste of her, the feel of her skin beneath his hands, his mouth. The way she moaned in the back of her throat when he pushed inside her. *Don't go there!* a voice shouted in his head, but he let the images play in his mind.

His gaze moved over her as she nestled like a kitten against the cushions, drawing her knees up and resting the mug there. She was beautiful, and just seeing her up close and not feeling the anger she often shot in his direction made the muscles in his chest tighten and his body hum with want. The images clouded.

"Okay, Detective, shoot. I mean, ask away," she corrected with a small smile.

When he didn't, she looked at him, frowning. "What?" Oh, those eyes are dangerous, she thought. His expression was dangerous. Lisa felt her stomach pitch with old sensations again. Her gaze lowered briefly to his mouth, and in one hit dead center of her heart, she remembered what his slow kisses did to her. Toe curling. Bone melting.

"I'm wondering why you're not biting my head off like last time."

She tamped down the feelings galloping through her body and said, "Trisha, my lawyer, made me see reason. You're just doing your job. The fact that you haven't charged me with anything speaks for itself."

Nash couldn't say that in his heart he didn't believe she was guilty, only that he was doing everything he could to find out who wanted her husband dead. He had to remain objective so no one would accuse him of crossing the line because he and the prime suspect had seen each other naked. In various positions. He shifted on the sofa. "I have to deal with the evidence."

"Which is enough to convict me." Her tone was flat. Hopeless.

"It's pretty strong. Especially adding this insurance payout."

"I didn't know he had the policy." When he looked skeptical, she said, "We'd been legally separated for nearly three years, so why would I know this? Did the lawyer have the policy all this time?"

"He possessed a copy, along with Winfield's will. But the original was in a fire safe."

Lisa frowned. "A safe in his office?"

Nash shook his head and wondered if she was playing him. Because if she was, she was damn good. If she wasn't, she was innocent as a newborn lamb. He prayed for the sheep theory. "The NYPD said it was in his apartment."

Her brows shot up and he had his answer. "*Our* apartment. We didn't have a safe. Where was it?"

"Behind a false wall in his closet."

She lowered her legs and propped them on the table. "I cleaned that place a zillion times and never knew. But then, I didn't have to clean his closet."

"I'm not surprised."

She paused mid-sip and arched a brow.

"Sheriff Walker did a profile on him. He was a neat freak," Nash said.

"I could have told you that."

"Tell me what you know, then."

He smiled as she rubbed one foot against the other. She was barefoot, her toenails painted. "Peter loved me." In his own odd way, she thought. "Almost too much."

"Was he abusive?"

"Did he hit me? No. And no man would and live." Her eyes flew wide. "Oops, I guess that was the wrong thing to say to a cop, huh?"

Nash smirked. "Just be honest with me."

"Are you implying I haven't been honest so far?"

"You haven't. Tell me what you fought about that night."

"I told you, it's private."

"It could be relevant to the case."

"It's not."

"Let me be the judge," he said softly.

"I thought you just gathered facts."

He gave a long-suffering sigh and rubbed his mouth. "That conversation is evidence."

"It's hearsay, so inadmissible." She set her mug down.

"That's your lawyer talking."

"Hey, she's right, you know. And she's good."

"If she's so good, how come you didn't divorce Peter till now when you left him nearly three years ago?"

"Lawyers get money for their services, and I couldn't afford to pay her. I told you this before, dammit." She pushed off the sofa, grabbed a cookie and bit into it as she paced restlessly before the cold hearth.

"Yet you could afford this house and business?"

She stopped and glared. "Yes, that's right. I was busy working two jobs and scraping together money for all this." She waved at the house and gardens. "Peter wasn't willing to give me a divorce, so if I wanted one right then and there, I'd have had to take him to court and fight him. I couldn't afford that. Not all of us were born with silver spoons in our mouths, a trust fund and a three-hundred-year-old pedigree, you know."

She popped the rest of the cookie into her mouth and chewed with a vengeance.

His features sharpened with anger, but she didn't care. "A place of my own and a means to survive were more important than a document that cut Peter officially out of my life." Lisa didn't think the final divorce would have made a difference to Peter. The night he'd died, he'd still thought there was a chance to win her back.

"Now you have two million dollars to do what you want with."

"I didn't want his money." If she did, she would have taken more than the clothes on her back with her when she left him.

Nash scoffed. "Are you telling me you'll turn it down?"

Her hands on her hips, she gave him a sour look. "Gee, Couviyon, as I don't think that's possible, no.

But I didn't kill him for it. I didn't know it existed. God, I can't believe you are digging at me over this.'' She rubbed her temple. ''It's only money, and while I thought money made a big difference four years ago, I don't now.''

While he'd grown up with every privilege, she'd struggled day by day to get her degree. ''Is that why you left me?'' The differences in their backgrounds were like night and day, he realized.

Her shoulders stiffened. ''I didn't leave, Nash. I was right here all the time. I broke up with you because we were going nowhere and I wanted more. End of story.''

''No, it's not.'' He set the mug down and stood, moving around the furniture toward her. Something inside him gave when she took a step back with that ''doe in the headlights'' look. He stopped. ''You just walked away.''

''Like hell I did.'' She'd stayed longer than she should have, long enough to get pregnant. ''You don't recall the conversations that mentioned marriage and kids because you ignored them, tuned me out, tuned out what I wanted. Then like an idiot, I made the mistake of telling you I loved you.''

Something yanked at his heart. ''That wasn't a mistake.''

''It was because you thought it meant I'd take crumbs till you were ready to give me more.''

''Crumbs? Jeez, you act like I used you.''

Her brow shot up in a smooth, angry arch. ''You

tell me, Nash. When did you ever in that year take me to Indigo Run? Introduce me to your brothers? Or even say to the other officers that I was your girl.''

Her eyes bloomed with unshed tears, and Nash felt the depth of her hurt down to his heels.

His features tightened. "Lisa, I know we didn't see eye to eye toward the end and—"

"That's the truth," she interrupted, not in the mood to rehash this. "Don't feel the sudden need to make it up to me, either." She moved to the door, opening it. When he just stared at her, she said, "I think you need to leave." *Before I do something stupid. Something I'll regret.*

Sighing with resignation, he gripped his notebook and moved to the door. She was always asking him to leave her life, he thought. He should've gotten the message by now.

"I don't think we should discuss our past anymore. Not till this investigation is over," she said, meeting his gaze head-on. He stood near, his aftershave lingering enough to tease her, his body radiating warmth she wanted so badly to feel again. And those eyes. Wicked blue and looking at her with a mix of sadness and want. She couldn't take it. Not when her heart continued to respond to him.

"We're linked by more than Winfield's death, Lisa. And not talking about us every time we see each other…well, do you really think that's possible now?"

"I'll give it the old college try."

"Well, I won't. But you should think about telling

me what you and Winfield fought over that night. Because if this goes to trial, you'll have to tell it to the world.''

She wouldn't. There was only so much more humiliation she could stand. "Good night, Detective."

He crossed the threshold and turned back to face her. "One more thing. Peter definitely died from a toxin."

"What kind?"

He flipped open his notebook. *"Convallaria majalis."*

Her eyes widened. "Lily of the valley?" she whispered, and the color drained from her face.

"You grow them, don't you?"

Her color returned with a vengeance. "Yes, and so does half the town."

"But half the town didn't make them into a tea for a bath."

"Neither did I, Detective. The killer did."

"You're certain the basket wasn't in the room when you visited Peter?"

"Yes, I'm certain. It wasn't there. I would have noticed it. And Peter would have made a big point about it, too. To him it would have been like my putting my wedding rings back on."

Nash nodded, said good-night and was still frowning as he walked down the steps toward his truck. If the basket wasn't in the suite after eight-thirty when Lisa was in the room, and yet had been delivered at six, where had it been between those times?

THE NEXT MORNING, Lisa thought Nash was like a bad penny, turning up when she least expected it. Now he was in the shop, questioning Kate Holling. The younger woman was flirting with him, she could tell. She decided to ignore them. At least she tried. But she was in the garden just outside the open door of the shop, and like a homing device, she was tuned to Nash's frequency.

On her knees in the nursery, she was digging a hole with a hand trowel when she heard Kate ask him, "Did I hear right that you and my boss used to have a thing going?"

"We're friends," Nash replied. "Miss Holling, where were you on the fifteenth?"

"I was here most of the day till about six. Then I went home and showered and changed to go out."

"Did you go out and what time did you leave your apartment?"

"Yes, I went to Masquerades at about seven-thirty."

Masquerades was a flashy, loud nightclub and always filled with the college crowd. Kate Holling was past college age.

"Till when?"

"About midnight. Need the names of some people who saw me?"

"Yes, I do."

There was silence for a few moments while Kate must have been jotting down a few names and phone numbers for Nash. Then Lisa heard her say, "It was pretty crowded, since there isn't much else to do in this town besides walk the waterfront, have ice cream and eat shrimp.''

Lisa shifted farther away from the door, out of earshot. She'd heard enough.

NASH COULD THINK of a hundred things to do in this town, but kept his mouth shut. Kate Holling was built and blond, with bright blue eyes that he suspected were that shade with the help of colored contacts. Her makeup was trendy, and though she wore an Enchanted Garden T-shirt and shorts, her hair loose, there was a hardness about her he couldn't put his finger on. While they'd talked, she fussed at the items close to the register or straightened plants that didn't need straightening. Nervous habit?

His gaze moved to outside, where Lisa was gardening. ''Thanks, Miss Holling.''

''Any time, Detective,'' she said, then spied something else to tidy and was off.

Nash walked down the side steps and into the fenced area of the garden. Lisa glanced up at him, shielding her eyes from the sun with one hand. ''She cleared?''

''Unless her story doesn't pan out, yes. Chris is cleared already. He was in Ollie's while his girlfriend waited tables. The manager verified it and didn't seem too pleased the kid hung around the restaurant all night.'' Nash surveyed Lisa's nursery, watching customers stroll the stone paths.

"I bet he had to keep eating to keep that spot, though," she said. "Ollie's does a great business on the weekends."

Nash didn't know why, but her garden made him smile. Land spread out around her house on the west side like a skirt, and instead of rows of plants, Lisa had sunk the pots into the ground in wild assortments, which gave the appearance that they'd been there all along. Shade plants sat under two spreading oak trees dripping with Spanish moss; flowers bloomed in the bright sunlight. A small fountain with glass and copper fairies gave music to the quiet. Enchanted Garden for sure.

"What about you? How's this going?" He gestured to the land.

"You think that I needed money enough to kill Peter?"

His gaze snapped to hers. "I've seen people die for a few dollars in their pocket. Greed is a great motivator and money changes people." Especially two million dollars, he thought. "But I asked because I care about you."

She scoffed and stood, shaking the dirt off her gloves and bending to collect her tools. She tossed them into a small wagon and pulled it along to another spot.

"Lisa, I do care."

Never enough, she thought. "Look," she said, pausing from unloading plants to fill the bare spots. "You care that I'm in trouble now, but Nash—" she struggled to keep the hurt out of her voice and wished she could let old feelings go ''—I've been here for months.''

''I know.'' Man, this was hard. Ignoring her these past months was protecting himself, and it told him he'd done exactly what she'd claimed. He'd only let her in so far. He'd let her into his memory once in a while, but seeing her again, being this close, was a whole new ball game. He wasn't sure either of them should step up to the plate.

''I can't trust you, Nash.''

He looked offended.

''I could say something casual and it could be held against me in a court, if it ever comes to that. I'd never know if I was talking to the cop or my old lover.''

Nash stepped close and looked down at her. ''I'm both, and you know that.''

''Hence, the no-trust thing.''

''Jeez, can you cut me some slack? You're the one who dumped me, you know.''

''So I'm supposed to feel bad and confess all to the detective?''

''Yes. No.'' He raked a hand through his hair. ''I got over it a while ago.'' *Liar.*

That stung, because she never did get over him. Standing this close, she knew it for sure. ''Good. Seeing anyone in particular?''

He frowned. ''No.''

''Still shying away from commitment, huh?''

His gaze narrowed. ''Still a smart mouth?''

She tipped her head and smiled. "Yes, I am."

Nash smiled. "Okay, cop talking here for a second."

She stiffened.

"I have a witness who said a basket from your shop arrived at 6:00 p.m. the day of the murder."

"Not possible. I only have one basket left, and it's in the storage room in the greenhouse." She gestured and started walking in that direction. "And I had no orders going out, so whoever told you that is lying."

"They aren't."

"Who delivered it? Mercury?"

"They're looking through files."

"Someone could have ordered it from me weeks or months ago and waited till now to send it, Nash."

"I've considered that."

"Come on." Dropping her tools on the ground, she walked to the greenhouse and went inside.

Nash felt instantly choked by the sweltering air and damp mist. Apparently unaffected, Lisa walked briskly to the rear and had to yank hard to open a second door. The release of the seal made items shake on the shelves. The small storage room housed stacks of black plastic pots, plant fertilizer and other supplies. There was one basket wrapped in plastic on a shelf.

"See, and here's the invoice." She grabbed the clipboard anchored to the shelf and handed it to him.

Nash scanned it, then flipped up pages to read beneath. According to this, she'd had only four baskets ordered in the past two months, and each one was signed out and dated. He nodded and handed it back to her.

She replaced the clipboard and moved to the door, walking back outside. Though it was over eighty outside, it was a relief from the humid confines of the greenhouse.

"I take it you haven't learned who the sender was, huh?"

"I have an officer on it."

"So what were you hoping? To trip me up or something?"

Man, that hurt, he thought. "No, Lisa, I was hoping for the truth."

She plucked her gloves from her apron and walked toward the wagon she'd left behind. "Think about it, Nash. If I were going to commit a crime, would I use anything that came from here?" She knelt and started digging. "How stupid would that be?"

"Very."

"But you still think I'm that dumb."

"No." However, making it blatantly obvious that they couldn't believe she was completely inept had occurred to more than one officer. Make everything point to her, and be neat and tidy, yet lack one facet— the killer instinct to take a life. Lisa didn't have it. He'd stake his reputation on it. Neat and tidy made cops more suspicious.

"Well, then, let's be up-front. I grow lily of the valley." She stood and walked several steps to the left and pointed at the ground. The little, white, bell-shaped flowers were in bloom. "I buy it from Cal Preston out near the highway, and I grow it in my backyard. It's often used for wedding bouquets or as a ground cover, and the last person I sold some to was your brother."

"Temple?"

"Yes, landscapers, gardeners, we're the same breed. So now you have more suspects. Mrs. Grady on Scott Street bought some the other day, too."

"Okay, I get the picture."

"Now there's a smart cop."

A phone sounded from somewhere in Lisa's apron. She scrambled in the pockets to find it, then hit talk on the cordless phone. "Enchanted Garden, how can I help you?"

As she listened, Nash watched her expression wither.

"No comment." She disconnected and stuffed the phone back in her pocket.

"The press?"

"Yes. The first call, but I expected it." She knelt to deadhead some flowers.

"Let me know if it gets bad. I'll ask a judge to put a gag order on it." Though this murder wasn't controversial, Nash had some friends in the right places.

She looked up at him, smiling genuinely for the first time since they'd met again. "Thanks, I think."

Her skepticism felt like a thorn under his skin, and Nash knelt to her level, needing to make something right in the mess of their past. Gazing into her wary eyes, he said softly, "Don't think, Lisa, *know*. I won't let you go to jail for a crime you didn't commit."

Her gaze searched his and desperation weakened her. "No, I suppose I always knew you wouldn't. I didn't do it, Nash."

"Then help me, baby," he said in a low tone she remembered too well. "What did you argue about with Peter?"

Her skin flushed and she held his gaze, refusing to speak.

He sighed and dropped his head forward. His fingers closed into a tight fist. "Okay." He pounded his thigh for a second.

"How about I take a lie-detector test?"

"Not admissible in court."

"But will it clear the suspicion I see in your eyes?"

Nash placed a hand on her bare arm. His fingertips worried her skin for a second. "It's just questions, you see, not suspicion. You have to trust me."

Lisa was still, the warmth of his hand on her tempting to iceberg inside her. It would be so easy to give her heart over to him. But she'd done that once before and still had the scars. She looked down at the Aztec grass, then grabbed it and popped it out of the container, effectively pulling from his touch.

"I trusted you once, Couviyon, and all you said was that you didn't want us to get so serious."

Nash's features twisted with guilt. God, he *had* said that. What a fool.

"My freedom might be on the line, but I'm not

risking my heart for you again.'' She met his gaze, her resolve crystallizing. ''So please be the detective I know you are and find out who killed Peter.''

JUST TO COVER all the bases, Nash paid a visit to the lily-of-the-valley grower, Cal Preston. The old man had skin like scorched parchment and wore dirty jeans and a sweat-stained T-shirt, yet Nash knew the Preston family had a lineage like the Couviyons. Fair Briar Plantation was as majestic as Indigo Run, the plantations flanking the town like sentinels.

But apparently Fair Briar wasn't holding up as well as Indigo Run, because the land looked overworked, and what should have been the front yard was rowed with plants. Not for the first time, Nash thought with admiration of how well his brother Logan had handled the family businesses. Keeping a plantation running when plantations were a dying breed was a skill that only one of his brothers—Logan—had.

Other than noticing that Preston was sporting a bruised cheek that was aging to yellow, Nash didn't discover anything useful.

''How'd you get that?'' Nash gestured to Preston's face.

Preston mopped his face with a bandanna. ''Slipping off the ladder in my greenhouse. What's it to ya?''

The man's stance and his sour attitude told Nash that someone in a local bar probably slugged him for shooting his mouth off. Nash showed him a photo of Winfield. "Have you ever seen this man?"

Preston snatched the photo, gave it a quick look, then handed it back. "Nope. He doesn't look like the kind who'd come all the way out here to buy greens."

Nash smiled. From what he knew about Winfield, Preston was right. "Thank you, Mr. Preston. Have a good day."

"I was," Preston groused, and walked back to the tractor he'd been running when Nash drove up.

With a twenty-page computer list of who purchased lily of the valley in the past year, Nash left, but he knew it was hopeless. Even his brother's company was on that list. And Quinn had told him it would only take a few sprigs to kill. That could have been snatched from any plant, anywhere.

And frame Lisa for murder.

Chapter Five

Lisa felt like a player in a game and she didn't understand the rules.

If she didn't figure them out soon, the ax hanging over her head was going to fall. She needed to do some prying and spying into her ex-husband's life. Nash wouldn't like it, but his freedom wasn't at stake.

She glanced surreptitiously at the guests in the Manhattan church. She and Peter had never attended church, which made her feel like a hypocrite. It was like sending a wedding gift to the girl who'd stolen your boyfriend.

The funeral service was like Peter. Reserved, attractive and just to the right of showy. Not a tear was shed, and more than a few people slipped out to answer cell phones. During the eulogy the participants spoke of Peter's talent for business, his drive, but not one person mentioned his personal qualities. And not for the first time, Lisa asked herself, *What were you thinking when you married him?*

Okay, he wasn't a total loser. He was smart, cultured, and he'd been sexy and fun those weeks he'd been vacationing in Indigo. He'd shown her the high-powered New York broker. And she, like a doe-eyed sap, saw only a chance to leave the small town with a handsome man and make the home and family she wanted. After losing Nash's baby a month after the breakup, she'd been emotionally primed for Peter's attentiveness, his claims of love and plans for a future. It was no one's fault but her own.

Her mama had warned her not to marry Peter, had said he was "deep under weird." Whatever that meant. Mama had a set of rules all her own, Lisa reminded herself. And in them, the only match for her daughter was one of the Couviyon brothers. She'd bet her newest watering wand that her mother wouldn't care which brother it was, either.

She winced at the thought and was glad her parents had moved to Florida and weren't in Indigo to witness the investigation. Eventually someone would blab, and she wondered how she was going to explain that she was the prime suspect in her ex-husband's murder.

Before she could dwell on that, the service ended and she headed for the door. The priest nabbed her, and Lisa groaned inwardly, but dutifully stood beside him to greet the mourners, trying to place them in her mind. Some she recognized from the past she'd shared with Peter; some she'd never met. All of them were fresh suspects to her.

Was the killer here? Which one of them hated Peter enough to poison him? And to set her up for the fall?

She didn't know anyone who hated her that much. Peter was another story. The man had no close friends, and she knew he'd made a lot of enemies.

People paused to offer condolences. After speaking briefly with one or two, she realized that none of them knew of their divorce. Which meant Peter had kept it to himself. As he had about the insurance. What had he been thinking? Peter had plenty of money, yet the cost of the premiums for the insurance had to have been through the roof. Where did he get the extra money? She knew he couldn't afford it unless he'd made some grand investment with a huge payoff in the past couple of years. Her lawyer had said the policy had been in effect since just after their marriage. Why had he hidden it from her? And worse, was there a policy like that on her?

Mourners filed past, each face more unfamiliar than the last. Then a thin man in an obviously expensive suit and inky-black hair that looked like a toupee stopped before her, grasping her hand and smiling sadly.

"Peter was a good man, a great broker."

Lisa frowned. "I'm sorry, who are you?"

He reared back a bit. "Carl Forsythe. I was his partner in a couple of business ventures."

"Successful ones?"

"Yes." He smirked as if she should know that. "You'll be inheriting his possessions, then? His personal files?"

Now that was a bit crass, she thought. "I don't

know the instructions of his last will." Not that Peter would have told her, she thought silently. "I'm not his wife anymore, Mr. Forsythe." She saw no reason to keep that secret; it would come out eventually.

He frowned, the wrinkles on his forehead growing more pronounced, but not moving the toupee. She had to force herself not to stare.

"We were divorced officially a week ago and legally separated for close to three years."

Forsythe's expression was nothing less than dull shock. A few others looked on with the same reaction, including a statuesque blond woman.

"Peter never mentioned it," Forsythe said. "In fact, he acted as if he'd found wedded bliss and it was going strong. He spoke of you often."

Okay, she thought, this was weird. A quick glance around told her the other mourners thought the same thing. "But I haven't been in New York for nearly three years."

Forsythe seemed about to say something, then cleared his throat and offered his condolences, instead. The blond woman approached, giving Lisa's clothes the once-over before offering a limp handshake. There was something familiar about her.

Something that put Lisa instantly on guard.

"Have we met?" Lisa asked, noticing the blonde's fake and bake tan that harshened the lines at her eyes.

The woman pursed her lips as if fighting a smile. "I worked with Peter. We were very close."

The possessive way she said that added to Lisa's suspicions. "Really? He never mentioned you."

I've seen you before, Lisa thought, and struggled to place her.

"He never mentioned that you were separated."

Obviously the woman was as impolite as Carl Forsythe and had eavesdropped on Lisa's conversation with him. "So," Lisa said, and folded her arms over her middle and regarded the woman as she would the compost pile in her yard. "Were you two in business together, or just in bed together?"

The priest glanced sympathetically at her, then took another step away.

"Business, of course," the blonde said haughtily.

Liar, Lisa thought. Not in the mood to argue with a stranger, she moved off, planning to leave. The woman followed, grabbing her arm. Lisa snapped around and glared till she let go.

"He never loved you, you know."

"Is that so?" Lisa countered. "Then why was he in my town a week ago pleading with me to stop the divorce?"

The woman's sudden anger slashed over her face. "You were just a pretty little Southern thing for his arm," she said, her tone degrading. "An ornament he could tame."

Lisa wasn't going to dignify that with an answer. She'd left him, which was proof that he couldn't tame her. Tired of this, she snapped, "Who *are* you?"

The woman's expression changed, as if she was

suddenly aware of something Lisa wasn't. "Catherine Delan." She neared, her height making her look like a polished amazon hovering for a potential kill.

Lisa went pale when she finally recalled where she'd seen the woman. "Your hair is different." The style was shorter, the shade lighter. Not that Lisa had seen much of her face before the woman went shrieking into the bathroom after Lisa had walked in on Peter and her having sex. Lisa hadn't seen her again after that, and now her gaze studied the woman, who looked at least eight years older than her. "And you know, darlin', you look better with clothes on."

"At least I had them off with him."

"You think that hurts, don't you." It didn't. And never would again. "You deserved each other." Lisa took a step past her.

"I deserved more."

Lisa jerked a look back over her shoulder at the woman. "Does that 'more' have a price? A nice round figure, maybe?"

Ms. Delan frowned and Lisa's suspicion magnified. The insurance would remain in probate and be awarded to Lisa, since she was the only beneficiary named. But that didn't mean Peter's will couldn't say differently. Lisa didn't care. That insurance only provided the police with a solid motive.

Lisa noticed that Catherine wore a designer suit and shoes, but also a cheap watch and faux diamonds, which any red-blooded Southern woman could spot.

Was she all facade, or had Peter paid for sex with more than his marriage?

"You should hurry home, sugah," Lisa said. "Your For Sale sign is missing." Lisa knew she was being snide. Yet the dig felt wonderful as she headed to her rental car, climbing in just as the skies opened up. She sat there, listening to the rain hammer the roof of the car, the teeny victory momentary and bringing back the humiliation of walking in on Peter and that woman in bed. Her first thought that day had been, *He wanted me to find them like that.* But she'd been visiting her family in Indigo and he didn't know she'd caught an earlier flight home. She'd planned to call him at work from the apartment. For on her trip she'd decided that they'd needed to separate or seek counseling. Peter had been too demanding, trying to rule every aspect of her life, and he crossed the line when he'd told her she couldn't go visit her "backwoods" family, as he called them. Less than a week later she'd walked into their bedroom and found him there with another woman.

The memory made her stomach pitch, and she viciously turned the ignition key. She didn't want anyone to know she hadn't been able to keep her husband from straying, but Lisa understood that Peter's infidelity would come out. Nash would know. And aside from humiliating her again, it would provide another motive for murder. Lisa swiped at the tears trickling down her cheeks and checked the traffic.

When she made to pull away from the curb, she

saw Catherine Delan still standing under the eaves of the church, fists clenched. From behind her, a hunched figure in a long, black coat rushed out into the rain and straight to a taxi. A coat? It had to be at least seventy, and sticky with the rain.

For a second Lisa watched the taxi, trying to see inside, but then she pulled onto the street. Her thoughts drifted to Peter and who'd want to kill him. Catherine Delan was at the top of her suspect list. What a piece of work. Hard, edgy. Not at all like the New York friends Lisa still had in this city. Though the embarrassment was still there, the affair didn't anger her anymore, only that Peter had lied to his business associates and a woman he wanted enough to betray their vows and share a bed. Their bed.

An hour later Lisa was sandwiched in New York traffic, chugging along foot by foot. A cab honked and she blinked, glancing at the street sign. She pressed the gas and made a right turn as she dug in the bottom of her purse for keys. She found a parking spot two blocks away and rushed into their old apartment building, then rode one of the elevators to the fifth floor.

In the hall outside the apartment, Lisa unlocked the door and pried back the police tape, then, realizing how many laws she was breaking, she took a breath and stepped inside.

Then she saw the destruction.

The elegant retro apartment was in shambles. Cushions were torn, lamps smashed. Drawers were not only overturned, but the bottoms shattered. The entertainment center was a pile of electronic debris on the floor. Not good, she thought, and turned to leave. She took two steps, reached for the knob, and pain exploded in the back of her head.

Stunned, her vision blurred as agony clawed over her skull. She staggered, then folded hard to the carpet. Her attacker shot past her. She glimpsed dark clothing before everything went black.

THE ELEVATOR DOOR opened and Nash stepped out just as the doors of the elevator beside it shushed closed. A warm fragrance lingered in the air as he strode to Winfield's apartment, slowing when he saw the half-open door. The police tape was still intact, but curling. He withdrew his weapon and nudged the door. His heart dropped like a stone at the sight of Lisa sprawled on the floor. Bleeding. He rushed inside, his gun close as he squatted to check her pulse, his gaze moving around the room. Alive, he thought, and searched the apartment for the intruder before coming back to her. Holstering his weapon and closing the door, he knelt beside her and checked her wound. Hurriedly he pressed a handkerchief to the back of her head and called her name softly.

She didn't answer and something vital and hard broke inside him.

He pulled out his cell and dialed 911, then called Detective Rhinehart of the NYPD. He didn't want the police to know she was here, but now he had no choice. He kept calling her name and held pressure to the wound for what felt like an eternity. She didn't stir and several worst-case scenarios tumbled through his mind. *Don't die,* he silently pleaded. *Don't die.* He checked the bleeding, then her pulse before he went to the kitchen. Grabbing a towel, he filled it with ice cubes, then rushed back, pressing the ice pack to her head. She stirred and blinked.

"Don't move."

Nash? "Oh, no." She groaned and reached for her injury, but he pushed her hands aside.

"Please don't move, baby. I don't know how bad it is."

"Like a hangover from a three day drunk bad."

"Should I be impressed that you know what that feels like?"

Despite the pain she felt herself smile. "No, it wasn't my most flattering moment." She rolled over, shielding her eyes with one hand and holding the ice to her head.

"Be still. The ambulance is on the way."

"Wonderful." Pain and now trouble.

"What the hell were you doing here?"

The bite of his tone rang like a bell. "Lower your voice. I'm hurt."

Nash battled sympathy for about two seconds. She could have been killed. "Don't give me that. You're at the victim's residence, injured, and the place looks like a hurricane swept through here."

"Noticed that, did you? Well, so did I. When I stepped inside, this is what it looked like. I didn't go beyond this spot, Nash. He got me right as I was leaving."

"He?"

"He, she, I don't know. He hit me from behind."

Nash looked around and saw the sculpture lying nearby, its base stained with blood. "The New York cops have been through this place already. They wouldn't miss anything. What did you think you'd find?"

"I don't know." She rolled to her side, then sat up. Her vision swam and Nash reached for her.

"Careful, baby, I've got you."

Lisa's heart nearly broke all over again right there. She gripped his arms. Because her head was spinning, she told herself, then gave up and pressed her head to his chest. He held her so tenderly she felt bruised by it.

"It was stupid, I know," she said. "But I needed to do something. I'm being framed for murder, Nash, and I can't just sit by and do nothing."

"*I'm* doing something, dammit."

"I know you are, but you aren't the one who's in trouble."

It might as well be him, he thought. For all his training, he felt helpless right now.

When she didn't say anything else, he asked. "Lisa, you still with me?"

"Yeah. I feel the need to sleep right now."

He was afraid she had a concussion. He tipped her

head back and stared into her eyes. The pupils were the same, a good sign. "Talk to me, then."

"You smell good."

He smiled with tender humor.

"I wasn't going to tamper with evidence or anything, you know," she said. "Just look around."

"For what?"

"I don't know. Something." She frowned, her gaze locked with his. "You followed me from the funeral service, didn't you?" He wasn't the one in the taxi, she thought. Nash, she'd recognize anywhere.

"Sure I did. I'm hunting for suspects, remember? And what the heck were you doing at the service, anyway?"

She searched his features, wondering if his tone sounded jealous only to her. Must be the head injury. "I thought it was the least I could do. Peter didn't have any family left."

"You didn't go to the burial?"

"Oh, there won't be a public one. It was Peter's request that no one attend that. I bet he didn't like the idea of anyone seeing dirt thrown on him or something." Lisa moaned with shame, and burrowed against his chest. "That was awful."

Nash tried to not smile.

"He'd have a cow if he saw his apartment now."

"What were they looking for?"

She didn't know if he'd meant to say that aloud. She leaned out of his arms, hunched as she pressed the ice bag to her head. "Files, maybe. Carl Forsythe asked me if I was inheriting Peter's files."

"The tall guy with the bad toupee?"

"Yes. Do the New York police have Peter's computer?"

"Yes, for all the good it's done them. They got around the log-in password, but haven't been able to get into encrypted files."

"Encrypted, like CIA spy stuff?"

Nash nodded.

"For the love of Mike," she said, rolling her eyes. "What do they need—a secondary password or something?"

He nodded. "They've tried for a week. Any ideas?"

She shook her head, then winced. "I'm going to be charged for this, aren't I?"

"No."

She eyed him. "You can't lie for me, Nash."

"I won't lie. I'll tell them you came here, not realizing the apartment would be secured, and found the door open and the place ransacked. When you were leaving, the perp hit you and left before I arrived."

"Nash," she whispered, lowering the ice pack. He pushed her hand back into place.

"You didn't touch anything. They don't need to know your intention. You just buried your husband, ex or not. Call it one last look at the life you had, I don't know. But I spoke to the NYPD just before I came up here, so they know I was headed here. And I do know that someone got on one of the elevators

just as I stepped out, because I heard the doors shut.''
He made a mental note to ask the doorman about that.

She felt her throat tighten, and if she didn't trust
him before, she did now. "Thank you, Nash."

He kissed her forehead and said, "Will you be okay
for a few minutes? I want to have a look around."
Nash's gaze swept the room, then he slipped his hand
into his pocket and brought out a pair of latex gloves
and snapped them on.

She started to get up.

He stood and pointed to the floor. "Stay, and keep
that ice on your head."

"But I can tell you what's different, what's wrong,
if anything."

He arched a brow. "You didn't know there was a
safe in your own home, Lisa."

He was right, dammit. "Fine."

She looked like a sulking child just then.

"This is what I mean about being helpless."

He smiled. "Darlin', you're anything but helpless."
He touched her cheek, then headed deeper into the
apartment.

Nash circumvented the room, noted the angry
slashes in the sofa cushions, the needlessly smashed
furniture and lamps. Even the shades were shredded.
There was broken glass everywhere. This was pure
unleashed rage, he thought. He also had trouble imag-
ining Lisa ever living here, in these rooms with sharp
lines and retro furniture. It was so unlike her home in
Indigo and reflected nothing of the warm, loving

woman he knew. As he made notes, he searched for the knife used to slash the cushions. It could have been any number of the ones scattered over the kitchen floor, and he realized that if whoever had done this had killed Winfield, then Lisa was lucky to get away with a knock on the head. If she'd interrupted this rage, she could have been stabbed to death.

He moved to the bedroom, stopping just inside the door. Other than a bottle of the only perfume Lisa wore lying on the floor and an open jewelry box beside it, virtually nothing was touched.

Except he'd found the knife.

Chapter Six

The butcher knife was embedded in the mattress.

Right through a cream-colored negligee that had been carefully laid out. The sight pushed a chill over his scalp and down his spine. Nash didn't doubt it was one of Lisa's nightgowns. He searched the dresser and found her clothes neatly folded in the drawers, some with slashes, some not. Lisa was never that neat, he remembered.

Winfield must have been obsessive to keep this stuff after so long. The bathroom was ransacked like the living room, yet woman's toiletries were still there. Lisa's? Or another woman's? He went to the closet, finding nothing unusual about Winfield's belongings that differed from how he'd found the victim's things in the Baylor Inn. Yet the garments were pushed back, the false wall and safe exposed. He looked in the adjacent closet and found what he'd expected. Women's clothing, slashed and scattered on the floor. He fingered a sexy beaded gown and tried to imagine Lisa wearing it and going out with Winfield. He failed.

Was his mind refusing to accept the image because they didn't fit, or was he just jealous? The woman sitting in the foyer bleeding was far different from the one this apartment portrayed, the one who'd married Winfield.

He returned to her just as the paramedics came down the hall.

Nash flashed his badge and they went to work on her. He stood back, watching, thinking of the nightgown and how the coroner, Quinn, had said that when Lisa left Winfield, she'd left everything behind. It must have been really bad for her to do that, Nash thought. Was Winfield harboring the hope that she'd come back after all this time? Is that why he kept all her clothing? Was that the reason they'd fought the night Winfield was murdered?

"It needs a stitch or two. She needs to go to the hospital," the EMT said. "Maybe stay overnight."

"No way," Lisa said.

"Yes way," Nash put in. "You could have a concussion."

"I have to get back home to work. I closed up for the day."

"I want a doctor to look at that first."

Lisa knew by his tone he was going to get his way.

Detective Rhinehart stepped in, looking around and groaning under his breath. He showed his badge and went to Nash. "She okay?"

"Yes, I am," Lisa answered for herself and Rhinehart smiled apologetically.

Nash explained to Rhinehart that he'd found her unconscious when he arrived, and Lisa listened to him tell the truth, leaving out one detail—that she'd come here to search.

Rhinehart nodded, taking Nash at his word. He questioned Lisa, advising her of her lack of wisdom at coming to this place. She agreed, hissing when the EMT put something on her wound.

"Does the rest of the place look like this?" Rhinehart said with a sour look around.

"Pretty much." Nash inclined his head to Rhinehart to follow him, yet paused to say, "Wait here," to the EMT helping Lisa sit on the stretcher. Two uniformed officers came in with heavy silver cases, one moving to bag the sculpture.

Nash and Rhinehart went into the bedroom, and the New York detective stilled at the sight of the bed. He radioed for a forensic team, then said to Nash, "My people stripped it, and the bedding is with our lab. The report should be in by the morning. Thanks for the files from Kilpatrick. Death by wedding flowers— cunning." Rhinehart shook his head. "This is your case, Couviyon. Your jurisdiction for the death, but I have a feeling evidence is staring us in the face that only a shrink can see." His gaze skimmed the room again.

"This is rage, look at the wild destruction that ends right here," Nash said. "And I'll bet that Lisa Winfield's prints were on the outside doorknob, not the inside. They weren't in the room at the Baylor Inn or on the basket containing the bath tea or, in fact, anywhere in the hotel room.''

"She could have wiped them off," Rhinehart said.

Nash shook his head. "Winfield was alive when she left. He bathed after she left. He would have seen her wipe them off. And if I know anything about this man," Nash said, looking around the room, "it's that he was obsessed with keeping his wife.''

"We have circumstantial evidence and motive."

Nash eyed the other police officer. "Mrs. Winfield was not aware of the safe or the insurance, and all the evidence can be placed in the hands of any number of people. She left him without taking so much as a cent or a piece of clothing. From what I've learned, she'd moved twice to avoid him in the past two and a half years.'' Nash didn't tell Lisa he knew that. She'd just see it as prying, not investigating. "She's given our offices everything we've asked for and agreed to a lie-detector test. It's all circumstantial, but that's convicted more than one innocent person. Background checks on Winfield pulled up the usual, and I'm still waiting on one that will go beyond his credit history. But I need more.''

"If we break his file codes, we'll have more," Rhinehart said. "A man doesn't encrypt files he wants the world to see. But right now we need Mrs. Winfield to identify the clothing. This could be someone else's.''

Nash didn't want to scare her, but like most things in this case, he didn't have a choice. In a few minutes he brought Lisa into the room. The way she clung to his arm told him that her injury was worse than she let on, yet when she saw the bed, she stiffened and inhaled sharply.

"Oh, God." She looked at Nash. "Is that directed at me?"

"Or another woman."

"Catherine Delan, maybe?"

Nash frowned at her as Rhinehart flipped through his notes. "The tall woman at the funeral?"

"She said she and Peter worked together and..." She swallowed, glancing between the two men, then admitted, "She said they were having an affair."

Nash noticed Lisa's rigidness, in her spine, her mouth. What else was beneath that look? he wondered.

"I've questioned her," Rhinehart said, looking at his notes. "She had some business dealings with Winfield, but didn't admit to more."

"Ask her again," Lisa said.

Rhinehart looked at her, his eyes sharp and judging. "You believe they were lovers?"

Lisa couldn't look at Nash. Peter had chosen Catherine over their vows, and Nash had chosen bachelorhood over her. She had so little dignity left. "I wouldn't know about recently, but...yes, she was Peter's lover. I haven't been in New York for nearly three years, Detective, but Catherine didn't know we were separated. Neither did Carl Forsythe. Peter led him to believe that we were still together. He had a thing about appearances."

"A thing?" Rhinehart asked.

"The best wine, the finest clothes. His tastes were expensive but it was all show, because he was cheap in other ways, like that bed. The mattress is from a bargain surplus dealer in the Bronx, but the frame is worth three thousand."

Nash's brows shot up and Lisa glanced at him, embarrassed to reveal this stuff, but she needed them both to see that the longer she knew Peter, the stranger he'd grown. "And with toiletries and household things, he'd buy in bulk and spend almost as much on a bottle of wine for a client. Or with phone service, he could have used two phone lines, one for the computer, but refused to do it. My clothing was designer, but most were a season off or from this nice secondhand store downtown. That—" she flicked a hand at the jewelry box spilled open on the floor "—is mostly paste and zircons."

Nash heard the sadness and disappointment in her voice, yet not for her dead husband, but for herself. Nash took some of the blame for that. He hadn't treated her much better than Peter had, keeping distance between them and then coldly cutting her out of his life when she broke up with him. As if she'd never existed beyond the dull throb she left in his heart.

"What do you know about his business dealings?" Rhinehart was primed to make notes.

She was quiet for a moment, her brow furrowing. "At first I knew everything, then later on he wouldn't talk about it with me at all, as if he figured I didn't know what mutual funds were and didn't need to know.'' A light seemed to switch on in her head, and her expression brightened. ''Before we split, or rather, just before I left, he was working on something that took him to New Orleans, but I don't know what it was. He wouldn't tell me about business, even when I asked.'' *And he'd patronize me when I did,* she thought, and for the first time considered that Peter had been doing something illegal.

Nash and Rhinehart exchanged a look and Lisa knew they were thinking the same thing.

''Sounds like he was living a double life, but not really risking anything,'' Rhinehart said. ''Which is odd for a man who risked other people's money on hunches.''

''Peter never did anything without a plan. He might have gambled on stocks, but not without a great deal of research. Impulsive behavior was not in his personality. I think marrying me was the only impulsive thing he ever did.''

''You don't think he loved you?'' Nash said, then wished he hadn't. He'd hate for her to have gone through all this and not feel loved.

''No, I know he did, or I wouldn't have married him,'' she said a little defensively. ''But he was different those first few months. I didn't really understand his compulsive behavior about order and appearances. It was a shock.'' At Nash's look, she said, ''Well, for pity's sake, the guy grew up on the streets. His father was a longshoreman, and his mother cleaned houses till the day she died. It's not like he was born with a silver spoon in his mouth.''

Nash blanched slightly, for that was the comment she'd made to him a couple of days ago. ''Maybe his tendency for control had to do with never wanting to have to clean up for a living. Or get his hands dirty.''

''I think his hands were dirty,'' Rhinehart said. ''Encrypted files means he was hiding something. We just have to find out where. And what.''

''Try Carl Forsythe. He asked if I'd inherit Peter's files, personal and professional,'' Lisa said. ''If they weren't in the computer or that safe, then I bet Peter had a safety-deposit box somewhere.''

Lisa's fingers dug into Nash's arm and he knew she was dizzy. He sent the other detective a meaningful look.

''Let's get this done and you to the doctor,'' Rhinehart said, and gestured to the closet and bath.

Hanging on to Nash, Lisa looked. Her gaze swept the room, recognizing everything she'd left behind. ''It's all mine. All of it. Good grief. Even my shampoo is still in the shower.'' This was what Mama meant by ''deep under weird,'' she thought, the sight of her shredded clothing making her see just how angry the person who'd ransacked the apartment was. And how deadly they could be.

She went back to the bed, staring at the knife thrust deep into the mattress and nightgown. ''This is the nightgown I wore on my wedding night.''

Beside her, Nash inhaled, almost glaring at the pale silk.

"It's safe to say that someone hates you, Mrs. Winfield."

She glanced at Rhinehart. "Bracket, please," she corrected. "Not Winfield. Not anymore." She looked back at the gown, remembering that night and thinking how she'd wished it was Nash lying next to her, wanting her enough to want a future with her. It had shamed her, and so she threw herself into being the perfect wife for Peter. But her efforts were never good enough.

Nash felt her squeeze a little harder on his arm and walked with her back to the foyer. The EMTs helped her back onto the stretcher. "I don't need this," she said.

He could see she was fighting a fresh wave of pain from just that short walk around the apartment. "Humor me, then, will ya?" He knelt and tugged on the straps. "I'll be down at the hospital in a few, after..." He gestured weakly at the abused home, yet kept his gaze on her. Her gaze shifted beyond him to Rhinehart. The man smiled gently.

An EMT put her purse on her stomach. Nash told her he'd take care of her rental car, and she gave him the keys, then pulled off her keys to Peter's apartment, handing it over with a look that said, *Yeah, I know I was stupid to come here, and you were right.* It didn't give him any satisfaction as they wheeled her out and to the ambulance on the street below.

Rhinehart gestured to a patrol officer standing outside. "Don't let her out of your sight," he ordered, and Nash knew the New York detective understood the significance of where he'd seen the knife.

Winfield's killer was dissatisfied and angry with Lisa. But the question why Peter Winfield was murdered hadn't been answered.

"The knife in the nightgown and bed was for her. Someone had to know she'd come here," Nash said. "And did you notice that none of Winfield's clothing was destroyed?"

"Yeah. You need to keep an eye on that lady, Couviyon."

"I will," Nash said. "The killer's going to realize very soon that she's not been locked up on murder charges and be even angrier."

"And maybe take it to the next level."

Nash had understood that the instant he'd seen the twelve-inch butcher knife embedded in the nightgown.

"I think we're looking for a woman," Rhinehart said.

"Not necessarily. This was all carefully staged. The perpetrator didn't expect to be surprised."

Nash jiggled Lisa's keys, then looked down at his palm. The apartment key was on a ring, a delicate silver disk attached. He frowned, flipping the disk over and reading the engraving. His features tightened.

"I think we've found the code," he said, and looked at Rhinehart, handing over the key ring.

On the silver disk were the words *Eternally Yours*.

THE POLICE GUARD in the hall outside Lisa's hospital room drew some curious looks. Inside, Nash was slumped in the chair, watching Lisa sleep. She was so still, and in the past few hours, Nash realized how easily he could have lost her. It twisted inside him, making him want to bash someone for doing this to her. Leaning forward, elbows on his knees, he rubbed his face, then looked at her.

Her eyes opened slowly and she met his gaze.

He straightened in the chair. "Hey."

"Hey yourself, Couviyon." She smiled softly. "What are you still doing here?"

"Confirming my theory that you snore."

"You liar." She pressed a button that made the head of the bed rise.

His smile was mischievous. "Hey, you're asleep, so how would you know?"

She sniffed. "I'm a Southern woman, and Southern women don't snore, sweat or drink. We nap, glisten and sip."

Nash smiled. "I stand corrected, ma'am."

"You've been here all night, haven't you?"

He nodded and Lisa was touched.

"Thank you. But really, Nash, you should go. I can take care of myself."

"I know, but I want to see you on a plane home."

"But I'm staying in New York. I can help."

"How? By getting your skull bashed in some more?"

"I can show you Peter's old haunts, his offices."

She threw back the covers and swung her legs over the side of the bed. Her head felt as if it had just blown off her shoulders, and she sagged into the bed, moaning.

"Told you so."

"Nobody likes a know-it-all, Nash." She crawled back under the covers, looking like a kitten burrowing.

He smiled. "Hungry?"

Her stomach rolled at the thought. "No."

"The doctor said you can check out anytime." Nash tapped the release papers sitting on the bed tray. "Detective Rhinehart was kind enough to send an officer to get your rental car and return it. And since your suitcases were in the trunk, I'm assuming you hadn't had a chance to check into a hotel before the services."

She shook her head. Pain bounced through her brain. She really had to stop doing that, she thought.

"Good, the bags are in my car, and after you check out, we're heading for the airport."

"Nash."

"No, Lisa. You're hurt and if you think your head aches now, wait till tomorrow. I want you in your home, guarded."

Her gaze shot to the door and the uniformed officer there. "Okay, this is getting scary."

"Which is why I want you home. This isn't my jurisdiction, and in Indigo, I can actually order people to protect you."

"You just want to be the boss." Her smile was

quick and slight. "What I can't understand is why me? I never did anything to anyone. At least not since I was in second grade and tied Patty Murkle's pigtails in knots."

Nash grinned. "What'd she do to deserve that?"

Lisa tipped her chin defensively. "Kissed Brewster Tate. He was my beau."

"Remind me never to tick off a seven-year-old." He stood. "So are you going to fight me on this?"

"No."

"When we know why Winfield was killed," he said quietly, "we'll know why someone wants to blame you." He gestured to the other chair. "There are your clothes."

She made a face. "You couldn't get me some clean ones?" These were stained with blood.

"Your cases were locked and our flight leaves in an hour and a half."

"Our?"

"I'm taking you home."

"I can manage alone. You need to stay here and question Catherine Delan and Carl Forsythe."

Nash simply folded his arms over his chest.

"Okay fine. Waste the taxpayers' money. See if I care." Yet she smiled up at him and whispered, "Thank you. Now get out so I can dress."

He didn't move, his gaze lingering on her curves in the ugly hospital gown.

She arched a brow, feeling the heat of that velvety look. "Don't you think you're taking the protect-and-

serve thing a little far?'' She made shooing motions
with her hands.

"Okay, I'm going.'' He turned to leave. "But, you
know, it's nothing I haven't seen before.'' He reached
the door just as a pillow hit him in the back of the
head.

"I FEEL SILLY.''

"You look silly,'' Nash said as he helped Lisa into
her house.

"Gee, so smarmy with the charm.'' She walked gin-
gerly toward the sofa; her skull felt as if it was going
to explode. "You know, if you'd been two minutes
faster with following me, I wouldn't be in this shape
and you'd have your perpetrator.''

He smiled at her. "Oh, yeah, sure, blame me for
your stupidity.''

"Why, Nash Couviyon,'' she drawled, her accent
sickly sweet, "you do know how to make a girl feel
like she's been rescued.''

He smirked. "I had to fight you to rescue you. I'm
a guy—I need to flex my muscles and growl once in
a while, you know.''

She snickered. "I'll have to remember that.'' He'd
been wonderful, she admitted. "Thanks for hanging in
with me, Nash. I know you had better things to do.''

"Not from my view,'' he said softly, giving her
hand a squeeze. "Come on, you need to rest.''

Lisa sank into the sofa. "I need to sleep. How are
you supposed to heal in a hospital when someone

wakes you up every hour to poke a needle in you or take vital signs?''

Nash hid a smile she wouldn't appreciate. She was crabby and in pain, and though she was teasing him, she was right. If he'd been faster, he could have prevented this. And if she'd been at that apartment sooner, she would have interrupted a killing rage.

The door opened and Nash turned, automatically reaching for his weapon when Lisa's assistant Kate came rushing in from the shop. She stopped short and Nash relaxed.

''Oh, my God, what happened? Lisa, you poor thing. You look awful.''

Lisa groaned. ''Well, it's safe to say I won't get a big head from too much flattery.''

''I'm sorry, but it's true.'' Kate cleared the coffee table, then propped Lisa's feet on a pillow. ''Can I get you some coffee, tea, anything?''

''No, I'm fine. Just watch the shop. You're in charge today. And thanks for coming in early to open up.''

Kate waved that off, pushing her hair off her shoulder. ''It's been slow but steady.'' She looked between Lisa and Nash. ''So who's going to give me the scoop?''

Lisa let her aching head sag back onto the sofa cushions. ''I—''

''She slipped and hit her head,'' Nash interrupted. ''It was an accident.''

Lisa kept her eyes closed, wondering what he was up to. "Heck of a funeral."

Kate frowned hard. "Yeah, I guess. Do you want me to help you upstairs or into something more comfortable?"

"I can manage alone, thanks."

Kate shrugged and said, "Call if you need anything."

"I'll be around," Nash said, and watched Kate head back to the shop.

"No, you won't. I don't need a baby-sitter and you need to go read reports, find some suspects. I'll be fine."

"Someone tried to kill you, Lisa."

"No, someone stopped me from seeing them in Peter's apartment. If they'd wanted to kill me, they'd have kept bashing."

Her expression was creased with pain, which was the only reason Nash didn't point out that the blow to her head could have killed her. Or mention the butcher knife in the bed. He went to her flight bag, unzipped a pocket and took out her pain medication. He left the room for a glass of water and came back to her, nudging her when she didn't open her eyes.

"Thanks." She took the pills, wishing for instant relief. She hadn't wanted to take them before the plane ride and force Nash to carry her through the airport like a sack of fertilizer.

"I'm going to get your bags."

She nodded, yawning her thanks, and Nash returned

to find her sound asleep. He set the bags down, shifted her into a more comfortable position on the sofa. She stirred. "You want to go upstairs?" he asked softly.

"Not unless you wanna come with me," she murmured in barely a whisper.

Nash's insides locked up. She was drugged, he reasoned. That sexy smile didn't mean anything. But the invitation lingered as he kissed her forehead, then took her bags upstairs. Her bedroom gave him pause, and he grinned.

Now this was Lisa, he thought, not like the bedroom in New York. This was comfortable and sexy at the same time. Daylight fell through the windows and twisted over the sheer fabric draped over the four-poster bed before pooling on the floor. The colors were vivid and warm, and plants filled every space she could find. Silks and cottons melted together in pillows, spreads, dust skirt, but Nash only saw her on that big bed, drowsy, her hair mussed and her arms reaching for him. He closed his eyes, set the bags down and made an about-face, then headed back downstairs.

You're asking for trouble, he warned himself, but he was beyond that because the instant he saw her asleep on the sofa, he wanted to kiss her. Hell, he'd wanted to do more than kiss her since she'd stormed back into his life.

The image of his partner's widow, destroyed and broken, intruded, and it put a grip on his emotions. He wasn't willing to risk Lisa's happiness like that. His job was dangerous; he had a scar to prove it. He didn't have the right to ask Lisa for more than friendship.

But dammit, he wanted to.

A COUPLE OF HOURS later, Nash left Lisa watching TV and bored out of her mind. He knew good and well the instant he was out the door she'd be in the garden, so he told Kate to call him and squeal on her. Nash checked in at the station, demanding the background checks on anyone associated with Winfield and hearing only that they were coming. Not fast enough, he thought, then read through a stack of messages and answered as many as he could.

One thing he learned was there were no deliveries made by Mercury to the Baylor Inn on the day of Peter's murder or the day before. So either the bellman, Mick, was lying or someone was masquerading as a Mercury employee. Nash figured it was the latter. The only person to see or hear Winfield when he was with Lisa was the housekeeper, Kathy Boon. Nash checked his watch. She'd be at work soon.

Room service, the housekeeper, the inn owner and the concierge all had access to the suite. Other than a passkey, no one could get in without being let inside, unless the killer locked the balcony door after he left. Nash needed more and knew where to look. He dialed Quinn Kilpatrick.

"Are those forensic reports in?"

"Hello to you, too, Couviyon. How was New York?"

"How did—? Never mind. Hello. New York is a big city with way too many people. I'm glad I don't live there. Now tell me you have news."

"All cop and no fun makes Nash boring as hell. Yes, I have news. We found blond hairs in Winfield's bedding."

"Blond?" Not red. Inside, Nash was screaming, *Thank God!* but he knew now that Lisa would never have let Winfield get that close to her.

"Yeah. There was none in the drains, and I'm doing a test now to confirm gender and if it's natural blond."

"You don't think it is, do you."

"Even I can spot roots."

"Dyed?"

Quinn's exasperated sigh came through the phone. "I won't know till I actually *do* the test, Detective."

"Sorry for the push, Quinn. But I'm not making much headway. Anything else?"

"The bath teabag was sealed with glue, not an iron as the brand calls for. So that tells me that whoever prepared it wasn't familiar with how to use it."

"Lisa couldn't tell if any were taken from her shop. She has a jumble of them and gets them off the Internet."

"How's our gal doing?"

Nash smiled to himself. Sometimes Quinn was like a mother hen. He told Quinn about the apartment and the knife in the gown.

"Sweet mother, if she'd been any earlier, she'd have interrupted that psycho."

"My thoughts exactly. I have a patrolman watching her house just in case. But she didn't see anything."

"Except stars, I'll bet."

Nash's lips tightened. Seeing Lisa on the floor bleeding was not something he'd forget anytime soon. "Call me when you have something."

"Good God, Nash, do you ever sleep?"

"Not if I can help it."

"Try it. You're testing your friendships," Quinn said, then hung up.

Nash wouldn't apologize. Not with Lisa's life on the line. He had to make life safe for her again. If for no other reason than allowing her to find a man whose job wouldn't put her in danger.

He was willing to take a bullet in the line of duty, but he wasn't willing to drag Lisa into his job. And inevitably, more than friendship would do that. He remembered clearly what losing David had done to his partner's wife, Laura. Even as Nash insisted to himself that he was restraining his feelings, that he was keeping as great a distance between them as he could, he knew it was a lost cause. Lisa was in his blood, and four years apart hadn't made a difference.

He should be smarter, he thought, a hell of a lot smarter. But as images of Lisa with someone else crowded his brain like ghouls in a kid's nightmare, Nash wondered if he was strong enough to let her go.

Chapter Seven

Driving to the Baylor Inn later that evening, Nash hunted down Mick. The kid was loading bags into an airport shuttle. "Mercury said no one delivered here the day of the murder."

"Well, then, someone's playing you, 'cause they were dressed the same as the Mercury riders." The teen shut the cargo doors and accepted his tip with a smile he didn't give Nash.

"This man you said who made the delivery, can you tell me—"

"I didn't say it was a guy."

Nash groaned. "A woman? That would have been helpful, Mick."

Mick had the good grace to blush. "Okay, yeah, it was a girl. She wasn't that tall, nice boobs and legs." He moved away from the front of the inn, lit a cigarette and took a drag, his expression thoughtful. He squinted. "It had to be a wig."

"Why do you say that?"

"'Cause it was dark and her eyebrows were light."

"You said she wore racing goggles."

"Not on her eyebrows."

Blond hairs, possibly dyed, in the bed and a woman with light brows was all leading him nowhere, Nash thought, frustrated. "Did you see anyone else just hanging around?"

"Yeah, Chartres."

Nash scowled. "The concierge insisted he didn't leave his office."

Mick smirked. "I don't know what stiff and pointy told you, but Chartres always makes the rounds. I've worked here for months. He's like a damn clock. Dinner at five before the guests, then he stops in with the housekeeper, the desk, even comes to me, as if we can't do our jobs without his tap on the shoulder, y'know? Then he strolls around to greet the dinner guests. If he stayed in his office, the chef would have noticed, because Chartres inspects the kitchen." Mick dragged hard on the cigarette. "Like Chartres knows the first thing about cooking. He gets excited when a guest sends a meal back to the kitchen."

Nash smiled, thanked the teen and made his way into the kitchen. The chef, a young, energetic man with a ponytail, confirmed what Mick had said. Chartres had indeed been in the kitchen interfering with the "creative process"; Nash could understand the man's irritation. The menu at the Baylor Inn changed daily. It was what made it so popular and reservations hard to come by. When the chef realized that what he said could get Chartres out of his hair, he told Nash more. John Chartres had been a concierge at a hotel in New Orleans and was fired. Why, no one knew.

Lisa said that Winfield had gone to New Orleans three years ago. It probably had little bearing on this case, but a couple of phone calls to the New Orleans police and Nash would know where Winfield had stayed and if Chartres was the concierge at the same time. Nash needed a connection. It was not quite time to visit Chartres again, he thought, passing the man in the reception area. Nash found Kathy Boon cleaning the room across the hall from the murder scene.

"Miss Boon?"

She didn't respond, her back to him.

He called again, then touched her shoulder. She whirled around, her expression taut. Then she sighed. "Hello, Detective. You startled me."

"May I speak with you?"

"I have a lot of work to do, so if you don't mind talking while I clean, sure."

"Did you see John Chartres on the upper floors the night of the murder?"

"You're sure it's murder, huh?" She swallowed thickly, glancing beyond him to the room still sealed with police tape.

"Yes, ma'am, we are. Did you see him?"

Her brow furrowed as she scrubbed out the bathroom sink. Nash noticed she wasn't wearing gloves this time, and her knuckles were scraped.

"He came up to remind me that room four was

occupied by honeymooners and to just give them towels and leave them be.''

"When exactly did you see him?" Nash asked.

"About seven, I guess. He was waiting for me at the storage closet on this floor."

"Wouldn't he just go find you, instead of waiting till you had to go back for supplies?"

"Yeah, I guess." Her brow knitted harder. "Yeah, in fact he was standing inside the open door. Maybe he needed something for one of the bathrooms downstairs.…"

Chartres didn't strike Nash as the fetch-and-carry type. "Isn't there another storage room down there for that?" Nash had the floor plans of the inn and knew there was.

Her features tightened. "Yes, there is."

Nash questioned her further and learned that William Baylor, the owner, had left late that evening. Later than he told Nash.

Nash stared at Kathy's hair for a second. She noticed.

"What?" She ran her scraped hand over her hair.

"Is that natural?"

After she got over her sudden confusion, she laughed uneasily. "What woman my age has natural hair color? Only the ones without gray."

"Gray? You don't look a day older than twenty five."

She smiled brightly and briefly gripped his arm. "Thank you, you made my day. I'm thirty-one."

Nash was stunned. "Would you be willing to give me a sample?"

"Of my hair?"

Even as she spoke she plucked out a couple of hairs. Nash put them in a plastic envelope.

"I'm not even going to ask why you want it," she said.

"I wouldn't tell you anyway," he replied, and thanked her. She barely acknowledged this last, turning on the tap to rinse the sink. Nash wondered if she was once a blonde.

"How did you hurt your hand?"

She didn't look at the scrape, covering it. "I—I caught it between the shelf and a box of soaps."

Nash had seen scrapes from brawls before, and this looked like one of them. He slipped his business card from his wallet and held it out. "If you ever need help, Miss Boon…" he said, and when she took it, he simply turned away, wondering whom she'd had to defend herself against lately.

Leaving the hotel, Nash returned to his office and hounded the rookie he'd assigned to do background checks on all the people who came in contact with Winfield. By six that evening, the young woman handed him a thick file. "I went back as far as high school on most of them."

"Good God," Nash muttered. He flipped through the file, nodding. "Excellent work. Excellent." She smiled brightly.

He thumbed through the files and called her back over. "Where's the one on Winfield?"

"I thought you only wanted suspects."

"The victim gives me the suspects, Officer. I need Winfield's. I needed it yesterday."

"Yes, sir." She snapped to attention. "Do you want what I have already?"

Nash nodded and she trotted to her cubicle, then rushed back with a file. "It's surface stuff, sir—credit reports, a few newspaper clippings, marriage license, job reevaluations."

It was more than he had, Nash thought as he thanked her and left the office. He was climbing into his car, intent on checking on Lisa before calling it a day, when his cell phone rang.

"You were right. I owe you twenty bucks," Detective Rhinehart said.

"The password worked?" Nash said, grinning. *Eternally Yours.*

"Yeah, now ask me what we found."

Nash listened, smiling. "I want to interview Carl Forsythe and Catherine Delan."

"I've already brought them in and questioned them, but I figured you'd want a crack at it. Before you ask, neither has a solid alibi for the time of the attack on Lisa. They insist they were in traffic from the funeral. Oh, yeah, the forensics are in on Winfield's apartment before it was ransacked."

"Let me guess—you found hair, bleached or dyed?"

Rhinehart was silent for a second. "Yes, in the drains and in the bed. It will take another day to confirm gender and if it is actually dyed."

"Science is too slow for me right now, and by the way, Lisa Bracket Winfield is a natural redhead."

"And you can confirm this?"

Nash heard the implications in the other detective's voice and felt heat creep up from his neck. "Yeah, I can."

Rhinehart chuckled. "I knew you two were friends."

"How so?"

"A man doesn't look at a stranger the way you did."

Nash cut the connection, tapping the phone against his chin. He didn't look at anyone the way he did Lisa. Because she was the one he wanted. Bad. Acknowledging that didn't put him any further away from his plan to let her go, he thought wryly. And though he wanted to see her and at least bring her an update, he didn't have time. He'd leave the officer watching her place and pray she was safe for the night.

He dialed the airlines.

LISA STIRRED, at once aware of the fog the painkillers left behind and that a noise had woken her. She lay still on the sofa, her gaze scanning the darkened room. She didn't need the grandfather clock in the hall to tell her that it was late. Past nine at least, she thought. Why didn't Kate leave some lights on? Even she knew better than to leave the lights off around the garden and shop at the west side of the house to deter break-ins.

She heard it then, clearer, the creak that could be a number of things, feet on her heart pine floors, a door opening, the house settling. She twisted from her prone position on the sofa and put her feet on the floor, ignoring the dull throb in her head and sliding her hand across the coffee table to the decorative iron rooster. She rose slowly, her gaze adjusting to the dark, the moonlight casting faint shadows of long-legged creatures on the walls. The little dot on the alarm didn't blink its usual glowing green. Damn. Why hadn't Kate set it when she left for the night?

Lisa walked slowly through the house, pausing to listen, then moved toward the shop. She hefted the rooster, aching to pay someone back and get in a good clobber. The noise came again. Once, twice. And behind her. She shifted away from the door to the shop, then down the back hall toward the kitchen. She switched sides, avoiding the beams from the oven light and the shadows she'd make.

Oh, jeez, someone's in my kitchen.

She inched around the doorjamb and saw a figure at the counter. The shadows and low light kept their identity hidden. With the rooster poised to strike, Lisa stepped inside and flicked on the light.

Kate whirled around, wide-eyed.

"What the hell are you doing here?" Lisa demanded, not lowering the rooster.

"My God, Lisa, you scared me to death!"

"I should have—you're in my house after hours. What are you doing here?"

Kate stepped to the side and showed the plate of food and a teacup on a perfectly set tray. "I was leaving you something to eat for when you woke up."

Lisa kept staring and Kate babbled.

"I'm sorry, Lisa, please don't fire me. I was closing up and you were still asleep, but all the lights were off. I didn't want you to wake up in the dark, so I was going to fix you something and then turn on a couple lights before I set the alarm. I was just trying to help. I didn't mean to frighten you."

Lisa simply stared, the rooster dangling at her side.

"Why are you looking at me like that?" Kate asked.

Lisa blinked. "Sorry, my heart is somewhere in my larynx, I think. You should have closed up three hours ago."

"I did, but I forgot to shut off the sprinkler system and came back. When I saw you still weren't awake, I thought of fixing this. There's herb tea on the stove."

Lisa glanced at the saucepan simmering the herbs. "Thanks. I appreciate it." Lisa let out a long breath and set the iron rooster on the island counter. She and Kate were not great friends yet, but Kate hadn't been working at the shop that long. The younger woman didn't care much for working with plants and preferred working the counter and shop, which was fine with Lisa. She'd rather be outside, anyway.

"It's okay. You can go home now. I'll lock up."

"You sure? You don't look so good."

Lisa shoved her fingers through her hair. She hadn't showered since the morning of the funeral, and she was still wearing the same bloodstained clothes from the attack. "I'll be fine. Thanks."

Lisa knew she wasn't being very cordial but seeing Kate in her house at this hour told her she wasn't watching her own back.

Kate grabbed her purse, told Lisa she'd shut off the sprinkler system and left. But not before pleading her case again. When Kate finally left, Lisa had convinced her she still had a job. Lisa reminded herself to get a separate lock for the door between the house and the shop. Her employees, no matter how much she trusted them, didn't need a key to her house.

She moved to the counter, peeling up the sandwich bread to see what lay beneath. Fat-free mayo, turkey and bean sprouts. How revoltingly healthy, Lisa thought, reaching for the cookie jar.

"WHAT IS THIS about, Detective?" Carl Forsythe picked at lint on his jacket sleeve, then looked up. He wore a bored look.

"I'll get to that in a second. How about some coffee? They have vanilla." Nash offered his best smile, holding up the pot. When the man nodded, Nash poured Forsythe a cup of coffee, asking if he wanted cream.

Forsythe shook his head and sipped from the paper

cup. Nash grabbed a chair, swung it around backward and straddled it. "So, Mr. Forsythe, where were you after Winfield's funeral?"

"Directly after? I was stuck in traffic."

Nash made a note. "Where exactly were you stuck?"

"Forty-second and Broadway for the most part."

Nash made another note, well aware that there hadn't been a traffic jam then. And it was less than six blocks to Winfield's apartment. "Thank you," Nash said, laying down the pen before looking at Forsythe. "So…you and Peter Winfield had been doing business for how long?"

"Several years."

"Successfully?"

"Yes, quite. Peter was a market wizard."

"Really? Then how come he wasn't swimming in cash?"

"He was a wizard for his clients. Insider trading is illegal."

"Yeah, I know that. So—"

Forsythe glanced at his watch. "I really need to go, Detective. Could you get to the reason for dragging me in here?"

"Sure, in a sec." Nash put up a hand, took a sip of coffee, then said, "What did he have that you wanted?"

"I beg your pardon?"

Nash made a show of looking at his notes. "Mrs. Winfield stated that at the funeral service you asked her if she was to inherit the victim's personal and business files.''

"And your point is?''

"Why would you want them? Now correct me if I'm wrong, sir, but a good businessman makes copies of all transactions.''

"I simply wanted to compare the accounting.''

"You think the victim cheated you?''

"No, but I don't trust a man who lies about his marriage.''

"Well now, that's a little strange since you didn't know about the state of the victim's marriage till you spoke with Mrs. Winfield at the funeral and she told you herself.''

"Yes, I did speak with her. And no, I did not know they were estranged.''

"Try divorced. Now tell me again why you wanted those files enough to confront the widow at a funeral?''

Forsythe was silent.

"Sir? Were you afraid he'd show them to someone? Did you want your hands on them first?''

"If Winfield was doing anything illegal, then I didn't know about it.''

"Okay, you can plead that you had no knowledge of the crime, but I gotta tell you, Mr. Forsythe, it's not looking good. Mr. Winfield kept excellent records.''

Forsythe's gaze narrowed. "Did he?'' His lips were pressed thin with anger.

Nash flipped open a file and scanned it, though he knew it by heart already. "They were hidden pretty deep in his home PC, but once we got the code... I see that you two corresponded on several occasions about buying MMG? Now what's that?"

"It's a plastics company."

"Hmm." Nash sipped his coffee. "That's why you wanted his files, isn't it, sir? To check up on the victim."

"Yes."

"You'd been working together in an effort to buy stock?"

"Yes."

"Then all this tells me it was an illegal transaction, Mr. Forsythe. Because the information Winfield had was insider trading within the company, using a fake corporation that was nothing more than a post office box."

Forsythe shut up, glanced at the two-way glass, then down at his coffee. He reached for it, but his hand shook and it never met the mark. "I want to call my lawyer."

"Certainly." Nash whipped out his cell phone and handed it over.

Forsythe used it, speaking hurriedly into the phone, then looking at Nash.

"I'll leave you alone," Nash said.

He left the room and went into the next, standing with Rhinehart. The interrogation room speaker was turned off. Nash watched Forsythe through the glass window.

"He's sweating," Nash said.

Rhinehart nodded. "He wouldn't tell us anything before, but then, we didn't know what to ask."

"You want a crack at him?" Nash offered.

"Nah, I like watching you pull out that 'I'm dumb as dirt' Southern charm."

Nash lifted a brow.

"Comes in handy, I'll bet, all that patience, slow talking. I'd be hounding him for answers."

"I'll teach you Southern speak if you like...suh."

Nash glanced at Forsythe, then stepped back into the room.

"Your lawyer going to join us?"

Forsythe looked up, paler than a moment before. "No, he wouldn't."

CATHERINE DELAN was flirting with Nash.

At least she was trying. She sat in the NYPD interrogation room, and crossed her long legs. Nash didn't bother to look, the woman was, if anything, obvious. Rhinehart watched them from the adjoining room.

"How long did you know Peter Winfield?"

"Five years."

"And your relationship with him was strictly business?"

"At first."

"Please go on," Nash said, leaning against the wall, his arms folded over his chest.

"He and I became lovers."

"Before or after he was married?"

"After."

"And?"

"And what?"

"Ms. Delan, Mrs. Winfield said you confronted her after the funeral service." He knew there was more than Lisa was telling him, and he figured she was just hiding her own humiliation.

"I didn't know he was separated from his wife."

"But that didn't matter to you. You continued to see him."

"Yes."

"Why?"

"I liked him."

"And how long did this go on?"

"It never really ended."

While he was asking his wife not to divorce him, Peter was sleeping with Delan. Talk about having his cake and eating it, too, Nash thought. "What did you do after you left Mrs. Winfield at the funeral?"

"I drove to the burial, then home."

"There wasn't a burial. Ms. Delan—it was Mr. Winfield's final request. Try again."

Catherine Delan's face flushed, then went pale and slack. She looked down at her nails, perfectly polished and shaped, as she spoke. "I drove around for a bit. I was very upset."

"Why?"

"Because Peter was dead!"

Grief or worry? he wondered. "What did you say to Mrs. Winfield?"

"I told her the truth."

"About what?"

"That Peter only wanted her as a trophy and that I slept with him."

"Why bother, Ms. Delan? She'd been separated from Winfield for nearly three years."

"She wasn't when she found us together."

Catherine's expression told him she hadn't meant to say that, and Nash kept his features blank. "Go on."

"Perhaps you should ask Mrs. Winfield."

"I'm asking you. Now."

"She came back from a trip early and found us."

Oh, God. Lisa. She was still married at the time. "So you confronted the widow on the day of her husband's funeral and reminded her that her husband had been unfaithful."

"She wasn't the widow."

"You didn't know that. As far as you were concerned, Lisa and Peter were still married. But that didn't matter to you."

Her hands clenched on her lap. "I suppose it was mean."

"What was your point in doing that, Ms. Delan?"

"She had it all."

"And you thought you could take it by sleeping with her husband?"

"No. And Peter came to me, Detective, not the other way around."

Nash pushed away from the wall and leaned his rear on the table, casual, but hovering over her. "Keep going."

"What? There's nothing to tell."

"You were having an affair with a married man and now that man is dead. Murdered."

Catherine Delan looked up, only half-stunned. "Murdered. And you think I had something to do with it?"

"I'm not accusing you of anything, Ms. Delan, I'm only trying to get at the truth."

She reached for her bag, pulled out a pack of cigarettes.

"No smoking."

She shoved them back into her bag. "Yes, she found us, but he didn't break it off with me. I thought she'd taken him back, that she was still around, being the perfect wife—because he never let her out to play, you know. Before then, whenever I did see her, she was dressed to the nines, dripping in jewels, and he stayed very close to her."

"And?"

"I thought she was still around, of course. Her things were in the apartment."

"You had sex with him in his own apartment, believing that he was still married and that was her home."

Catherine Delan looked ill.

"Did you love Peter Winfield?"

"Not really."

"Either you did or did not."

"No, I didn't."

"Then why the affair? To hurt someone you didn't know? Because Mrs. Winfield had married him?"

"No. I just…"

"Yes?"

"I had other reasons. I can't tell you."

"Ms. Delan, a man has been murdered and you were the last one to have intimate contact with him. That makes you a suspect. A prime one."

She paled further. "But I was sleeping with him to get the chance to search his files!"

Why didn't this surprise Nash? "What for?"

"Peter had damaging information on a friend of mine—a good friend."

"You were sleeping with him for nearly three years and hadn't gotten hold of the files in all that time?" Nash tried to keep the disgust out of his voice and failed. "What was Winfield doing with this information?"

"Holding it over my friend, what else?" Words died when she realized she'd implicated herself.

"Who's your friend?"

"I can't say."

Nash moved to the door.

"I haven't done anything illegal," she cried. "You can't hold me."

"Blackmail is a crime, Ms. Delan. So is knowing about it and not bringing it to the attention of the authorities. It's called 'intent to conceal a criminal act.'

And I can hold you for twenty-four hours. There's meat loaf on the jail's menu tonight. Hope you have the stomach for it.''

Nash called for a uniformed officer. When the man appeared, Nash spoke to him in hushed tones with his back to Catherine Delan. The cop looked past him to the woman.

"Okay, fine," Catherine said. "I can't tell you the name, but Peter *was* blackmailing this person. He had evidence about some trouble from a couple years ago and this person wanted it back."

"Not good enough. I need a name, and yours will do for the prosecuting attorney," Nash said.

She looked at him, her eyes sparking with fury, then she snapped, "Chartres. John Chartres."

Chapter Eight

"Don't listen to a thing that man says, Lisa. I knew him when he was wearing diapers."

At the sound of Nash's voice coming from the front of the nursery, Lisa looked up and smiled. Then she glanced at Temple.

The younger Couviyon brother just shook his head and groused, "Older brothers are the bane of my existence. They take every opportunity to embarrass me."

"Then just tease them about being older," she said with feeling. "Believe me, it'll catch up with them."

Lisa watched as Nash moved along the stone path toward her. With each step, she felt her heart pick up a pace. She was at the far end of her land with his brother Temple, counting off plants being loaded onto a truck, so it was a long way and a lot of heart jumping till he got close. Lord, she loved the way Nash walked. His strides were long, lazy with a hip-rolling gait that reminded her of a cowboy. As if he didn't have a care in the would. And she knew he did. He'd been in New

York, and though she hadn't seen him in three days, it didn't take but one day for her to realize she'd missed him more than was wise. For both of them.

"Hey, old man," Temple called, then winked at Lisa.

"Old means wiser, too, you know," Nash replied.

Temple's gaze shifted pointedly to Lisa, and Nash felt his insides clench at the subtle reminder. *If you were so wise, how come you lost her?* He hadn't done anything to keep her, Nash thought. Now he'd spent three days away from her, trying to sort out his feelings, and though he thought he had them neatly packaged again, looking down at her, he knew he didn't.

"Hi there," Lisa said, wondering if the breathiness in her voice was her imagination.

"Hey yourself. Should you be working out in this heat?" he asked, touching the back of her head and taking a peak at her wound.

Instinctively, she covered his hand. "It's okay, just a little tender is all. Don't worry so much." The motion brought his face closer.

"I do more than worry," he said gruffly, bringing his gaze back to hers. For a moment he just stared, a recognition spiriting through every cell of his body.

"Thanks for the patrolman," she said, her gaze flickering to the road beyond the fence.

"The person who hurt you is still out there."

"I still think it was just so I didn't see him."

"And the butcher knife in the mattress slipped your mind?"

A pearl of fear dripped down her spine. "Oh, yeah," she said stupidly.

Nash smiled, yet not willing to concede her safety for a moment.

"Okay, Lisa, that's it," Temple interrupted, earning him a glare from his brother. "Got a total?"

"Yes, sir, I do." She picked up her clipboard and handed it over to Temple.

"I heard you were looking for anyone who grew poisonous plants, like lily of the valley, and pennyroyal," Temple said to his brother as he glanced down at the list of items.

"Yes, but it grows everywhere and it wasn't a viable lead."

"That's good, since the Baylor Inn has lily of the valley. Right alongside the café patio, if memory serves."

Nash frowned. "*You* planted it there?"

Temple nodded, put his signature on the account, then handed the clipboard back to Lisa. "About a year ago, yes. It was a request of the owner, William."

"Why request it?"

"He seems to think it was grown there years ago. Wanted it back."

Nash was still frowning when his brother got to his feet and signaled his workers to leave. The truck pulled away and Temple looked at Lisa. "Thanks, Lisa, your stuff is always the best."

"It's a compost thing."

Grinning, she ignored Nash's shocked look when

Temple leaned down and brushed a kiss across her cheek, then whispered for her ears alone, "Don't step into those waters again unless you really want to, darlin'. I'd hate to have to punch out my own brother."

Lisa met his gaze, searching his handsome face, and felt a little needle of worry prick her. Temple flirted with her every time she saw him, but she never thought much of it. He flirted with every woman, young and old. Was he sweet on her? Or was he just being a protective friend?

Nash stepped close. "Go to work, youngun."

Temple hid his smirk in a smile as he left. Nash noticed Lisa watching Temple stroll away. He wasn't sure he liked that she enjoyed his brother so much.

"What did he say to you?"

She glanced at him, waving at Temple as he got into his SUV. "Huh? Oh nothing important."

Nash frowned again. That look was too sweetly innocent for him. "He's a playboy, Lisa."

She laughed shortly. "Oh, don't I know it. Half the women in this town have shared his bed or want to, including my employee." She reached for her cart handle.

Nash flushed for his brother's sake. "How about you?"

Lisa whipped around. "I can't believe you asked that."

"You didn't notice that he was flirting with you?"

"He always does, but he's just a friend *and* your brother, for pity's sake."

That made Nash feel a little better. "I know and I'd hate to have to bash his face in."

Now she really laughed. "You two think more alike than you know." She turned toward the house, loving that he was jealous. Peter had been obsessive and hovering, but not what she'd call jealous. In fact, he *wanted* her to talk with anyone who'd benefit his career. She'd been a useful ornament, nothing more. In some ways Nash had done the same thing. She'd been a constant date, a lover, but nothing beyond that. And it still stung, because she'd never felt for Peter what she felt for Nash.

Walking beside her, pulling the second cart, Nash watched her expression, saw the hurt there and wondered what she was thinking.

Suddenly she looked at him, her brows knitting. "You found something in New York. With Delan and Forsythe?"

"More than something." He checked his watch. "But I'll talk to you about it later, okay?"

Lisa didn't like the way he avoided looking at her. "What's the matter?"

He hesitated for a moment, rubbing his mouth. "I've learned some things about your ex-husband that aren't flattering."

She scoffed. "I bet you I could tell you more."

"I wish you would."

She stopped, her hip cocked. "If this is about the conversation we had the night Peter died…" Now she hesitated, opening her mouth, then snapping it shut and sighing. "I'll have to think about it," she finally said. It would bring back so much more than just an argument between ex-spouses. It would open a door to her past she'd thought she'd firmly shut when she left Nash. Was she ready for that?

"At least now you're thinking about telling me."

He inched closer as she spoke, hemming her in, crowding her. The look on his face was tender and patient, and she tried not to remember what it was like to be with him and feel that tenderness when he'd made love to her. It was the one thing that had stayed with her with amazing clarity.

"You're not accusing me of killing Peter anymore. Think that might have something to do with it?"

"Maybe," he said on a smile. "Can I call you tonight?"

Surprise sparked, along with pleasure. "Yeah, sure. How about when you're done with work you come over for supper?"

"I don't know if that's wise."

"It's an ethics thing, right?"

"No, it's an 'I don't know if I can keep my hands off you' thing."

Heat ignited deep inside her and rushed to explode. "Is that what you want, Nash? Only to put your hands on me?"

The question slammed home and Nash heard all the reasons and excuses he'd told himself the past few days to back off and let Lisa go. But he was confused and his heart wasn't listening to logic and reason. And of course, he was assuming a great deal. Assuming that Lisa felt the same as he did. With her, he could never tell. If he could, he would have seen their breakup coming, instead of being broadsided.

"Not only my hands," he said with a crooked smile. "But do you know what you want from me?"

I've always known, Lisa thought with heartbreaking detail, but that was four years ago. With Nash close, staring at her the way he had years ago, Lisa felt torn. She wasn't sure her heart could take losing so much again. She didn't trust it. "I'm not sure anymore," she said, and knew that if she wanted more, she'd have to tell him about the child she lost.

"Then hands will do for now." Gently with a featherweight touch, he put his palms on her waist and tugged her closer. "For now," he said in a warning tone, and the air crackled between them. He leaned and brushed his mouth across hers.

Lisa's breath hitched and her knees softened. A rush of feelings swept through her like warm seawater. "Nash."

He met her gaze and waited. For her reaction, for an indication that she wanted more. He didn't even know what *he* wanted from her. He checked himself and said, "I have to go." Yet he didn't move.

"You aren't gone yet?" She smiled.

He stole another light kiss, wanting to hold her closer, taste her more deeply. Not yet, he thought. He had to have patience. Because Lisa had hidden more than the fact that her husband had been unfaithful. She was hiding the pain of it.

He stepped back, his hand lingering on her waist for a second before he strolled away, leaving her flushed and confused, and then at last, smiling.

NOTHING IN THIS LIFE felt better than putting pieces of a puzzle together, Nash thought as he stepped into the concierge office of the Baylor Inn.

Chartres didn't hear him and he waited till the man noticed. It wasn't long. He snapped around from looking at his computer and Nash enjoyed a bit of delight in watching the man's face pale to a pasty white. It made his slicked-back black hair stand out further against his skin.

"Can I help you, Detective?" Chartres said.

"Would you like to add anything to your previous statement about the night Winfield died?"

Chartres's Adam's apple bobbed in his narrow throat. "What do you mean?"

"You lied to a police officer and concealed information that was pertinent to this investigation."

Chartres's expression bled with resignation. "My past with Winfield had nothing to do with his death."

"Perhaps, but withholding information is a crime."

Nash stepped inside the office and didn't take a seat. Instead, he stood over Chartres and stared down at him. He detected the faintest quickening of his breathing.

"What was between us was past, buried," Chartres said.

Oh, it was buried all right, Nash thought. "Why don't you tell me about Winfield and why he would come all the way down here to see you."

Chartres was taken aback. "He didn't. He was here for some other reason, and when he recognized me, we had words." He rose and went to the door, closing it softly, then faced Nash.

"On the night he died?"

"Yes. Briefly. Winfield was blackmailing me."

"Go on."

"We met in college, and when I landed a job at the Artisian Hotel, he visited. He said he was there on business. He asked for a favor, a woman for the night, and I obliged by finding him one."

"Was this the first time you'd done this for a guest?"

"No, it wasn't. New Orleans, even in the Artisian Hotel, is where people like to shed their inhibitions. Accommodating guests was my job," he said with a hint of pride. "I'll admit that it got a bit out of hand."

"What was your take?"

"I beg your pardon?"

"Don't get all righteous, Chartres," Nash said sourly. "You were running hookers in the most prestigious hotel in New Orleans. You risked your job and your future. Pimping is a crime."

Chartres made a face. "That's so vulgar. My girls…" Chartres clamped his lips shut, realizing what he'd said. "The women were clean and lovely and cultured. They had to be—it was the Artisian."

"I don't care if they were society debs. What did Winfield do about it?"

"He threatened to reveal what I was doing. Unless I paid him. I did at first. But his demands increased and finally I couldn't pay. He whispered things in the right ears, and I was fired."

He said it all with a methodical litany for reciting high school poetry, without feeling, lacking details.

"What did you do about it?" Nash asked.

"Nothing. I'd lost my position and had no more income. His source, as it were, dried up."

Nash already knew he'd sent Catherine to Winfield's bed to get that blackmail evidence back. "What did he say to you when you saw him here?" Nash asked.

"He remarked that my employer obviously didn't know about my past, and he'd take pleasure in telling him. It was a threat to start making me pay again. See, when I lost my position at the Artisian, I'd lost my reputation, as well. And I refused to pay because I couldn't. Baylor knows, by the way."

"Charitable of him to give you a job."

Chartres reddened, then folded his hands on the desktop. "And how did you learn all this? Winfield played everything very close to the vest."

"I'm not telling you that." Winfield had photos of women, dates, times and how much Chartres was paying him.

For a second Chartres searched Nash's face, then said, "Did you know about Carl Forsythe? That bald idiot made millions with Peter, illegally, and Peter kept good records. Very good ones. Even recorded phone conversations. He was paranoid, thorough and obsessive." Nash saw Chartres's face pale and the man realized Winfield had kept the same records on him.

"I'm aware of that. How did you know about Winfield's dealings with Forsythe?"

"An old friend mentioned seeing them in New York."

Nash liked it when he knew a whole lot more than his suspects. "And you've known this person how long?"

"Catherine Delan? Oh, years."

"Before New Orleans?" Nash asked, and heard the trap close.

"Yes. We met in the Artisian—" Chartres clamped his lips shut. "That little witch."

Nash stared, knowing Chartres had just linked himself to Peter Winfield, Catherine Delan and Carl Forsythe.

Chartres sagged back in his leather chair and shook his head. "She said she'd do anything for me, that she loved me."

"Your first mistake was believing that. Your second was sending her to sleep with a married man who was richer than you."

Chartres melted into the chair, rubbing his forehead.

Catherine had been doing Chartres a favor, in the beginning, by sleeping with Winfield and trying to regain the blackmail evidence that Winfield had documented. Pictures, payoffs, contacts. And Catherine Delan couldn't get the stuff because it was in Winfield's computer under an encrypted file. She had as much to risk and gain. Because Catherine Delan was an alias, and she had a rap sheet for prostitution. She'd been one of Chartres's "girls."

"Winfield paid for other women, Detective."

Nash felt anger rise through him like a slow storm. Damn Winfield. "Give me names, Chartres." Nash simply stared and waited, knowing it made Chartres nervous.

"He asked for a hooker in the best hotel in New Orleans, Detective. I doubt it was the first time."

It was easy to deduce that Chartres wanted to throw suspicion off himself, but in Nash's eyes the man had the biggest motivation, not to mention the best access, of anyone else implicated in Winfield's death.

Nash flipped through his notes. "You told me that deliveries are signed for and delivered by the hotel. However, the bellman said that a delivery was made at 6:00 p.m. The day of the murder."

"So?"

"Mick has no reason to lie, nothing to gain, yet you didn't want anyone to know about your relationship with Winfield and your pimping for hookers at the Artisian."

Chartres inhaled sharply.

"You told me that deliveries were signed for," Nash went on. "This one wasn't. You also spoke with the chef, criticizing his meals, and strolled through the dining room. Then you told me otherwise and made a signed statement to that fact." Nash had confirmed this before leaving for New York, but he had needed more evidence to make Chartres a suspect. Time and place was key. And he had both.

"I spent most of the time in my office. I left only for a moment."

"Yet you lied about it," Nash restated. "You were also seen at the storage closet on the second floor at around six-thirty. Why?"

Chartres frowned. "I don't know what you're talking about." He started shuffling papers.

"A witness puts you outside the storage closet."

Chartres looked thoughtful. "I was there to remind the housekeeper, uh, Miss Boon, not to disturb the honeymooners."

"Chartres, how long do you think you can dance this tune?"

"Till this is over, I didn't kill Winfield."

Nash wasn't getting anywhere with Chartres and was afraid that no one would till he was on the witness stand. "Where were you," he asked, "at 4:00 p.m. on the twenty-first?" The time of Lisa's attack.

Chartres looked at his calendar. "I was overseeing the inn's contribution to the Shrimp Festival, which is next week. I had to meet with the other local businessmen on Baylor's behalf."

"Witnesses?" Nash said.

Chartres gave him a short list, his hand shaking a bit.

Nash folded it into his notebook. "Don't leave town." Nash needed the smoking gun to arrest Chartres.

"I have no intention…" Chartres's eyes flared as the impact of what Nash had said hit him.

Nash moved to the door, then paused and looked back. "One more question. Do you know what type of flowers are growing in the gardens surrounding the inn?"

Chartres looked confused. "Yes, a few, but Mr. Baylor would be better at pointing them out than me. He's aware of every flower his family has grown for the past hundred years."

Nash felt anger slip up his spine. He'd assigned the job of gathering information on Baylor to an officer. Nash was going to have his badge for letting this slip.

Nash started back out the door. "Where is Miss Boon right now?"

"Gone, Detective."

Nash heard the smugness in Chartres's voice before he turned and saw it in his face.

"She vanished."

"When?"

"She was here at work today and disappeared in the middle of her shift."

"And you didn't think to alert me?"

"I am now."

Nash had the urge to haul the prissy little man to jail just on principle. "Why did she leave?"

"She didn't say. In fact, she didn't say much at all. She just left her cleaning cart outside a room and walked away."

Good God, did Kathy Boon fall victim like Peter? "Did anyone see her leave?"

"No. And yes, I asked. She must have slipped out the servants' entrance."

"I thought those doors were locked."

"If she was inside the room, you can open them from in there," Chartres said.

Nash left the offices, leaving a message for Baylor that he wanted to see him, then learned where the service cart and Kathy Boon were last seen. He moved through the vacant room and slipped out the back French doors. It was a lower level, below Winfield's room. He stepped out, careful not to disturb more than necessary. There were small footprints in the dust leading out the door, yet only the forward portion, as if the person had been running.

He returned to the hall and started questioning the guests. There were only four occupied suites on the floor and all guests had been asleep when Miss Boon was working her shift.

Great, he thought, dialing the police station. Now he had a missing person.

And no one seemed to care but him.

THE WARM BREEZE rolled off the river and across Lisa's backyard. Nash sat opposite Lisa at the patio dining table, unable to take his eyes off her. Which would be wise since he'd missed his mouth a couple times already. Above her, tiny lights twinkled softly through the arbor.

Lisa seemed nervous, avoiding anything that had to do with Winfield's murder. He didn't blame her. It wasn't exactly polite dinner conversation.

"You're looking at me that way again, Nash."

Relaxed back in the chair, he sipped his wine. "What way is that?"

She tossed down her napkin. "Like you're trying to figure me out. Stop it."

"You're too complicated to figure out. I gave up years ago."

Sadness slipped briefly over her features, then was gone. Lisa stood, gathering dishes, and Nash joined her, carrying bowls and platters into the kitchen. His attention was locked on her shapely behind, and he almost tripped and shattered her grandmother's china.

"Dinner was great, Lisa, thanks."

"You're welcome, but we're beating around the proverbial bush, Nash."

"Okay, fine. You want me to ask, I will. Why the hell did you marry a man like Winfield?"

"He was handsome, wealthy, and he loved me."

"But you're so…opposite."

"Yes, I know. We didn't exactly have a long engagement, and the minute I put his ring on, he changed.'' She shrugged, as if it didn't matter anymore.

But it did. She'd made a big mistake with Peter. At the time, she'd still been freshly wounded from losing her child. She thought, like a fool, that she could make the pain go away by loving another man. It didn't. It was the wrong man, she thought, looking at Nash and feeling a wild stab through her heart.

Nash realized he wasn't going to get more than that and he switched gears. ''The night Winfield died you were in his suite.''

She nodded, rinsing dishes. ''And we argued.''

''About what?''

''You.''

He stilled, then finished putting the plate in the dishwasher while she started a pot of coffee.

''Why me?'' Any other time he might be flattered.

''Well, not exactly you to start. But it always ended up about you.''

''Wait a sec. Back up a bit.'' He waved. ''Tell me first—why did Winfield want you back when he'd been cheating on you?'' Her skin flamed with color, but Nash wouldn't let it go. ''Why would he beg you not to divorce him even after papers were signed and he was—''

''—already sleeping with Catherine Delan?'' Lisa turned, leaning back against the counter. The coffeemaker sputtered behind her. ''For Peter it was power. Peter didn't want *me*. He just didn't want anyone else to have me. Especially you. It was about control, like he had with his clothes, the apartment. And other people. I had to move more than once because he wouldn't stay away, and the police wouldn't do anything because I hadn't divorced Peter. And he hated that I was back in Indigo.''

Nash listened, hearing more than she was saying as the words poured from her.

"He liked that I was poor but educated, that I was attractive and had a Southern accent. I honestly think he came to the South just to find me. Or someone like me.'' She shrugged. "He sure as hell didn't like the South that much."

"Why would you say he came to find someone like you? He loved you."

"Yes, I believed he did. In his way. In the end he traded love for obsession, but he certainly showed his love in the first months. But as you saw by the apartment, it got a little weird."

"Before he was unfaithful?"

Her embarrassment colored her features. "Yes. I'd returned early from a visit here—"

"I remember when you were here," Nash interrupted. They'd met on the street outside a shop and he'd been ice-cold toward her. He'd regretted it half the night. "Was that the reason you went back to New York early? Because of me?"

"Partly, yes, but I was tired of my mother telling me I'd made a mistake. She'd warned me. Mama never liked Peter. You were her favorite."

Nash smiled gently.

When the coffee finished brewing, Lisa turned and filled two cups, adding cream to hers, black for Nash. He took it and sat on a stool. He noticed that Lisa couldn't be still, moving around the kitchen for fresh plates, then pulling an apple pie from the fridge.

"Well, I'd come home to sort things out. Seeing you didn't help, but I knew I had to make my marriage work. I'd already lost you." She sliced and served the pie. Neither touched it.

"You're the one who left me, Lisa." The words came softly without recriminations.

Her expression deepened with sadness. "Oh, Nash, you were already gone. When your partner was killed, you just...dried up." He'd gone from kind and interested in her, to apathetic and distant. She'd felt like a fixture in his life and very insignificant.

Her eyes burned, and Lisa looked everywhere except at Nash, then took a sip of her coffee. It scorched the back of her throat. It was better than the ache working beneath her heart like a sharp spike.

"Anyway," she said on a deep breath, "I got home early and walked in on Peter and Catherine."

For a second Lisa looked wounded and betrayed, and Nash felt it from across the counter. She pushed at her hair, her hand trembling, but Nash knew Lisa. She was trying to hide her hurt from him, to be brave and act as if the past few years weren't a living hell.

"Lisa?" he said. "Look at me, honey."

She did and lost the battle, choking, covering her mouth. He came to her, took the cup from her hand

and set it aside, then wrapped her in his arms. She clung fiercely to him, and Nash closed his eyes, a thousand *what if*s floating through his mind. All he wanted to do now was soothe her, erase the pain.

Lisa moaned, digging her fingers into his back, inhaling his scent, feeling safe and…home. "I—I didn't recognize Catherine then. Or at the funeral." Very softly she said, "What kind of person does that make me that I even spoke to her?"

"A shocked person," he whispered, and she leaned back and met his gaze. "Let it go, she's not worth it."

Lisa nodded. "I know. It was her hair. It was longer and darker, but that's no excuse."

Nash frowned. The hairs found in Winfield's suite were bleached with dark roots. But his attention shifted when Lisa stepped out of his arms. He felt suddenly cold and empty. He wanted her back in his arms so badly, he shoved his hands into his pockets to keep from dragging her to him and kissing her till her pain went away.

"So what was the argument about?"

Lisa met his gaze and marshaled her nerve. "I still refused to stop the divorce. There wasn't anything I could really have done at that point, anyway, not that I'd ever change my mind. When he finally understood, he was livid, and that made him mean. He didn't hit me or anything. But he said I was never good enough to be his wife, that he'd tried to mold me, but I was too stupid to understand that he was the best thing that ever happened to me."

"God, what a pig."

"Yeah, well, that was nothing new to me. When I was leaving, he tried to touch me and I think he got my scarf in the process. The next day I wanted it back. I didn't want him to have anything I loved."

She was quiet for a moment, her gaze steady and locked with Nash's.

"How did your argument end up on me?"

"It was his last dig. Always the same. That I should be grateful for what he'd done. Hadn't he picked me up off the ground and dusted me off, made me into something? Hadn't he given me more than Nash Couviyon would?" She laughed to herself, but there was no humor in it. "Hadn't he loved me when you wouldn't?"

"Aw, Lisa. I'm so sorry."

She blinked, looking defensive. "Why? It's not your fault. It's mine. Those were my choices. I'm not blaming you." She picked up her coffee and started to drink, then made a face and poured it into the sink, leaving the cup there. She gripped the edge of the cold porcelain. "My mistake is not your fault, Nash. I know it and you should, too."

Those *what if*s were goading him again. "Okay, let's leave that for now, but tell me, did I make you feel like you weren't good enough for me?"

She turned to face him. He was close, too close. "Yes, sometimes."

She looked so small right now, he thought. "For

that I'm ashamed and sorry, and I didn't see what I was doing,'' Nash said.

"You didn't see a lot."

"We didn't want the same things then." *Do you now?* a voice in his head asked. *Don't you want a future with this woman?*

"I know. Funny thing, neither did Peter. He said he did, but all it took was seeing him with children to know he thought they were dirty little creatures other people only tolerated."

"You really want kids, don't you."

Her smile was soft and melancholy. "I wanted a future with a man I loved. If kids came, then great." She shrugged. "But I'd had my chance and lost it."

"With Peter."

Lisa swallowed, knowing it was now or never. "No, Nash, with you."

"What do you mean?"

"Before I broke up with you, I'd asked you where our relationship was going. You said you didn't want to get serious."

"Yeah, I did." She'd told him she loved him then. For the first and last time.

"Then after our breakup, you cut me out of your life like I'd never been there. You wouldn't even speak to me. That hurt the most. It was as if all we'd had, the love I had for you, meant nothing."

Nash searched her features. "That's not true. God, do you know how much it hurt just to look at you? It was killing me, Lisa. I was destroyed and shocked. I didn't know how good I had it with you till you were marrying Peter.''

''Oh, God,'' she moaned, her lip quivering and crushing his heart. ''I wish you'd said something, anything.''

He searched her face. ''What are you trying to tell me? I can see it in your eyes.''

''I'd needed you so badly then, Nash.'' Her voice cracked. Silent tears spilled.

''Then why did you leave me?''

''Because you didn't want a future with me, and I was already carrying your child.''

Chapter Nine

"You were pregnant with my child when you left me?"

The accusing way he said that was something she'd expected. The disgust in his face, she hadn't. "Yes."

"Damn you, Lisa." He took a couple steps away from her. "How could you keep this from me?"

How dare he? she thought. "Why don't you take a second and think back four years ago." He glared at her. "Think," she insisted. "You were still stiff from the bullet wound, your partner, David, was dead and you sure as hell weren't letting me any deeper into your life."

"You should have told me."

"Why? You'd already made your feelings quite clear. I asked you if you wanted to be married someday, to be a father. You told me very angrily that I shouldn't expect any more from you, 'so don't go making wedding plans, baby,' I believe were your exact words."

"I couldn't see any future, Lisa." Furious, he

pushed his fingers through his hair. "My partner was dead and I saw how devastated his widow was."

"I know that. I was here, remember? Laura and David were my friends, too."

"But I couldn't protect you from that kind of pain."

"News flash. I didn't ask you to protect me. I'm a big girl, Nash. But the point was, you never wanted marriage and a family before David was killed, so don't blame it on his death. You'd already made up your mind. I wasn't going to tell you about the baby then. You think I'd want you if you were only doing the right thing?"

The phone shrilled. Lisa snapped it up and listened. "Yes, he is," she said, then shoved it at him as she walked past into the living room.

Nash watched her go, glaring at her back, shaking inside, then put the phone to his ear. "Couviyon. Fine. I'll be there. I said I'll be there!" He hung up and went into the living room. Lisa was sitting on the sofa, her knees drawn up, her gaze locked on some far-off point.

"I have to go," Nash said.

"Figured as much."

"Lisa, we need to talk about this some more."

"It's done, Nash. Our baby is gone and so is that part of our life." Her voice fractured and Nash felt the strings suspending his heart give a little. He wanted to stay badly, but there wasn't time to talk. He walked to the door.

After a moment she followed.

He paused, gripping the knob, anger and something else Lisa couldn't name crimping his features. She felt all they'd gained recently withering before her eyes.

"What was I supposed to do, Nash?"

He glared. "Tell me. Let me help you."

"Why? To force you to marry me? You're a gentleman. You would have," she said before he could. Her gaze raked his features, her heart splitting bit by bit. "Oh, Nash," she said, her voice weakened with pain, "I didn't want you that way because you'd made your feelings clear. About me, about any future. When I lost our baby—"

He flinched, in his eyes, his shoulders, and his grip on the door latch.

"—I already knew I was alone."

He simply stared, his face wiped clean of emotion, then walked away. "You didn't have to be alone, Lisa. That was your choice."

Lisa closed the door, fighting renewed anguish. *I shouldn't be hurting like this again,* she thought, then she folded to the floor and cried.

THE NEXT MORNING Nash was still angry enough to chew nails. Snapping at anyone who crossed his path, he barely noticed the other officers giving him a wide berth, but when he barked at his friend Quinn Kilpatrick, he knew he was in trouble.

He couldn't tell anyone what he was thinking or feeling because he didn't know himself. All he could think for the past few hours was that Lisa had been pregnant with his baby and she'd never told him. If she hadn't been accused of murder, if her ex-husband hadn't been murdered in his town, he might never have learned about it.

But she told you. She didn't have to.

Why? he wondered. Was she trying to hurt him?

She was right, he would have married her, but he was honest enough with himself right now to admit that he wouldn't have been happy about it at the time. That was then, he thought. *You were a jerk to everyone.* And the only thing he could see was David's wife, Laura, utterly destroyed by her husband's death, and himself putting Lisa in that position.

Would a baby have made a difference then?

He rubbed his face. Leaving Lisa alone with a child was worse than leaving her alone, right?

And yet, because he'd let her go, she'd been alone these past years, anyway. Years they could have shared.

As the day progressed, thoughts of Lisa wore him down to the point that his skin felt as tender as his mood. He wanted to see her and, well, yell some more, he thought as he stood in William Baylor's office, waiting. When Baylor stepped into the office, the innkeeper couldn't cover his surprise fast enough.

"No one told me you were here, Detective."

"That's because I didn't announce myself," Nash said, waiting for Baylor to take a seat.

"What is this about?"

"Lying to the police." Nash dropped a file on the

table. Baylor looked at it, then him. "Peter Winfield was trying to buy your hotel."

Baylor, small and wiry, seemed to wither slightly in the leather chair. He stared at the file. "Yes, he was. I wouldn't sell. This home has been in my family for centuries."

"Why did he even attempt it?" Nash asked. Winfield had contacted Cal Preston at Fair Briar Plantation, too, Nash had learned earlier.

"He insisted he wasn't buying it for himself, but for his wife. She was to be a silent partner."

Nash didn't waste a moment. He slipped out his cell phone and dialed Lisa. When she answered, he felt the hole in his chest gouge deeper. She sounded tired, worn-out. He asked her about the sale.

"Absolutely not," she said on the other end of the line. "He never mentioned it, nor would I have agreed. I wanted no more ties to him, Nash."

He thanked her and cut the connection, knowing his abruptness only made the rift between them wider. "She denies it."

"You're going to believe a murder suspect?"

"Mrs. Winfield is no longer a suspect. She's never lied to the police." Nash's gaze pinned William Baylor to the chair. "And she has given us all information we've asked for."

She has now, Nash thought, knowing that the one conversation he'd been wanting to hear about had been about him, with Winfield making Lisa feel small and unworthy.

"I'll need you to amend your statement, Mr. Baylor."

"Yes, of course."

"And call yourself a lawyer. I'll be back with a warrant to examine your personal and business files."

Not waiting for Baylor's reaction, Nash left the office, striding through the hotel toward the reception area. John Chartres was at the front desk, and only his gaze shifted up as Nash paused to get his bearings. Chartres nodded slightly, the look smothered in smugness, and Nash scowled. The man's butt was in the sling, so what did that look mean? Nash headed back to his office.

He passed Lisa's place. Cars lined the street, and he caught a glimpse of her in the garden area, talking with a customer.

He ground his teeth, trying for calm and reason. And to see things from her side. She'd been pregnant and scared when she knew he wouldn't be receptive to the idea of a baby, he thought. He wasn't exactly her champion then, either. Last night after she'd told him, Nash recalled the conversations they'd had four years ago. She'd been subtle then, and since he was so wrapped up in the loss of his partner and not wanting to put Lisa in Laura's position, he hadn't heard what she was trying to say to him. Maybe, though, he hadn't wanted to hear her. *Love me or I'm leaving.* And when he'd told her he wasn't ever considering more than the here and now, she'd looked out for herself and cut the ties between them. Then she'd suffered losing their child alone.

Alone.

He should have been there. And the loss of what he never had felt like a lead jacket coating his heart.

As he parked and went into the police station, part of him was still furious with Lisa for not telling him about the baby, yet knowing the truth didn't make a difference now. Their child was gone. But he was just as mad at himself for not listening to her. For not seeing she was hurting. For tossing her love away. What are you willing to do to get it back? he thought. And could he?

The phone startled him from his thoughts. He fought the urge to growl and tried for a polite "protect and serve" tone. The caller was Kathy Boon.

Nash immediately motioned to an officer to trace the call. He'd been searching for her. She'd been using a fake driver's license and name.

"I was worried about you, Miss Boon. You disappeared." Nash sat in his chair. "Are you all right?"

"I just wanted to tell you that I had nothing to do with that man's death."

"How can I be sure?"

"You can't. But I didn't even know the man, Detective."

"I need to see you, speak with you again. You're a witness to Chartres's whereabouts."

"That can't be helped," she said, and Nash noticed that her voice sounded as if she was covering the phone so as not to be heard. "I told you all I could," she whispered. "I can't come back. I won't."

His patience snapped. "Ma'am, your name isn't Boon and your driver's license is a fake, so why don't you tell me what's going on? Maybe I can help you."

"*No!* No," she added a little more calmly, then said, "This isn't your problem and you can't help me. You'll only get hurt, Detective. But Cal Preston, the man at the Fair Briar Plantation, had nothing to do with this, either."

How did she know he'd questioned Preston again? Fair Briar Plantation had been on Winfield's list of properties to look at for purchase. And Preston had refused to sell, too. Did Winfield think that giving Lisa property was the way to get her back?

"Why should I believe you?"

"Preston made a pass at me when I went there for a job and I decked him."

Nash wanted to smile at that, but his concern was for the terrified woman on the other end of the line. Bracing his elbows on his desk, Nash held his head in his hand. "I can protect you."

"Forget me. No one can." The line went dead.

Nash looked over at the officer.

"It's a cell phone. Nearest location we can get is Macon, Georgia. A truck stop on 95."

Good God, did she realize how dangerous that was? "Send her picture to the tri-state area, and alert the Georgia Highway Patrol." Nash slipped out a copy of her photo and handed it to the officer. "Whoever she is, she's in big trouble."

And too scared to come to the police.

LISA OPENED her door and smiled. Her buddy Hope Randall held up two pints of ice cream and spoons. "Comfort food," Hope proclaimed, then inclined her head toward the street. "Cute patrolman, should we ask him to join us?"

Lisa glanced past Hope to the unmarked car that glared in the darkness. "He's too young for you."

"No man single and over twenty-one is too young, honey." Hope pushed her way inside the house. "Come on, you sounded awful on the phone. You practically begged for this ice cream and the extra pounds it'll bring. Let's talk. Or rather, you talk. I'll listen and commiserate that all men are jerks and we women are far superior beings."

Smiling, Lisa snatched the pint of ice cream as she passed, broke it open and had a spoonful in her mouth before Hope found a seat in her living room. The ice cream tasted heavenly. And Lord, she'd missed her best pal. A private investigator and bounty hunter working for a law firm, Hope had been injured working on her last case, and as soon as the doctors said she could, she'd treated herself to a two-week vacation in the Caribbean. Right now, Lisa wished she'd gone with her.

"Okay, spill. How was Grand Cayman Island?"

"Expensive, sexy and with more rich men with off-shore bank accounts than any single woman my age should be allowed near."

Lisa grinned. "Meet anyone?"

Hope sent her a sly look. "I'm not the kiss-and-tell type."

"Hah! Since when?"

"Since now."

"Ahh, find Mr. Right?"

"Mister I-know-how-to-seduce-and-leave-a-lasting impression, but no, not Mr. Right."

"You never know."

"He hasn't called, so I know." Hope held a scoop of ice cream before her mouth and asked, "So what about Nash?" She shoved the spoon in her mouth and moaned over the taste.

"What about him? I told you, he left here yesterday evening and I've heard from him once and it was police business."

"He's the police, and you are his business right now. I consider this progress."

Lisa made a face.

"What are you going to do about it?" Hope asked.

"Nothing. Why should I?"

"Want me to do some snooping on this case?"

"I can't afford you. Besides, if Nash can't find anything, how could you?"

"I don't have the restrictions he has and I'm a woman. Show a man a little skin and he's putty."

Lisa laughed.

Hope shrugged. "Do you love him?"

"Don't know," Lisa said around the ice cream. A voice in her head screamed, *Would it hurt this much if you didn't?*

"Yes, you do. You loved him once, Lisa, you can fall back into it again."

"Let's not forget that I loved him, but he did not love me. Besides, too much has gone on. Peter, the baby…" She let that hang since Hope could fill in the blanks herself. She knew everything.

"Don't get so hopeless. Give the guy some time, for heaven's sake. His reaction was normal, you know. Shock, hurt, feeling a bit betrayed."

"You said that on the phone."

"It bears repeating."

Lisa took a deep breath, the pint sweating in her hands. She jammed the spoon in and shoved more into her mouth. "Whose side are you on, anyway?" Lisa asked.

"I love you both. But lets face it, Nash wasn't exactly the open-door kind of guy. Dark and mysterious will only get you so far."

"He's not mysterious. Not to me at least. I know he's mad at me and he's dealing with it in his own way, but if he can't get past it, then that's just… tough."

"Is it really?"

"I broke up with the man because I didn't want to trap him into something he didn't want. I don't see how that's changed. Besides, I just got rid of one husband."

"Careful who you say that to, sugah," Hope said, her attention on the pint she was emptying faster than Lisa's.

Lisa paled. "Oops."

Hope stopped eating long enough to push her hair off her shoulder. "He believes in you."

"He believes I'm innocent, *not* that I haven't betrayed him by not telling him the truth." Lisa started to scoop up more ice cream, then tossed in the spoon and set it aside. "Okay, fine, I'm afraid."

"Of what?"

A bolt of pain shot through her heart, and she inhaled. Their child was gone, long gone, but Nash was hurting now as she had. *And now he's blaming me for it.*

"That this will never stop hurting and if I let myself go, I'll just get kicked in the teeth again." Lisa felt tears burn her eyes and she didn't want to cry. Dammit. She'd had enough of this. "This stinks."

"Yeah, it does. But Nash wears a white hat, Lisa, more on the inside than out. He might have been closed off before because of David's death, but that was a while ago. Give it a chance," Hope said.

"I'm not ignoring him, he's ignoring me."

"Then I say again, what are you going to do about it?"

"Fight?"

"Now that's the Lisa I know."

"YOU HAD A CHANCE to look at that?" Standing in the doorway of Jack Walker's office, Nash nodded at the preliminary report on the sheriff's desk.

Jack looked up, frowning. "You look like hell, Couviyon. Get in here and close the door."

"Didn't sleep well last night. The report?" After closing the door, Nash dropped into a chair.

Jack rose and turned to the coffeemaker, fixing Nash a cup. "Didn't sleep at all from the looks of it."

Nash took the cup and sipped. Though Jack and he had been good friends for years, he was still his boss and Nash didn't want to talk about Lisa with him. At least maybe not till Nash cooled off.

"I've looked at those reports till they just blur into a gray mess." And he wasn't concentrating, either. He wanted to go see Lisa, but finding Winfield's killer took precedence over his personal life. *What life?* he thought cynically, and swallowed a mouthful of coffee. "I'm missing something, something small."

"You never miss a thing," Jack said. "And yeah, I read the reports. Talk."

"The doors to Winfield's rooms were locked from the inside. There's an outside staircase leading up to Winfield's room, but no one occupied the lower room that night, and it was locked. No one saw anyone going up the staircase and the footprints are small but inconclusive. If Winfield did let someone in from the balcony, then it was someone he didn't want anyone to see."

Jack nodded, absorbing. "The hair-fiber test back? Do we know if it's a man or woman?"

Nash shook his head. "Not yet, but I'm betting it's a woman. Winfield was having an affair with Catherine Delan. For some time."

Jack winced. "Lisa know?"

"It's one of the reasons she left him. Now, the scarf around the neck and the tidy manner of death, well, a man would have done something more violent."

"Unless a man wanted it to look like a woman did it."

"I've thought of that. This person was smart. We don't have a single print other than Winfield's to lead us anywhere. Everything used can be linked to a dozen people aside from Lisa. Winfield knew his killer. No struggle, no forced entry. I'm betting he welcomed his killer inside the room. And with the hair fibers found in the bed, it wasn't the first time. All I can prove is Catherine Delan didn't take a flight here. If she drove, it's a hell of a long way, and she didn't strike me as a woman who would go out of her way to do anything for anyone, even murder."

"Chartres had the most to avenge," Jack said. "Blackmail, losing his job at the Artisian. He was okay with Delan sleeping with Winfield to get his blackmail evidence back. Add that to pimping in New Orleans, and we know the man uses women."

"He was furious that Delan had talked to the police."

"Sure, she was his worker bee. And that she hooked for him confirms that he's a user. But what's that got to do with Lisa Winfield?"

"Lisa was the perfect target," Nash said. "Chartres had feelings for Delan, none for Winfield, and he didn't know Lisa."

Jack leaned back in his chair, the wood and leather creaking as he propped his cowboy boots on the desk. In jeans and a pale plaid shirt, Jack Walker looked more like a farmer than a sheriff.

"But did he know about the insurance policy?"

"He won't admit to it. But then, Lisa didn't know, either. All Quinn found under Winfield's nails was lily-of-the-valley oils, so he didn't claw at his attacker. The ligatures left by the scarf were postmortem. As if the killer wanted him more dead than he already was."

"The apartment that was ransacked, what about that?" Jack asked.

"It wasn't ransacked, it was destroyed. It was rage, Jack. Passion. The knife in the mattress says revenge to me. And I think whoever killed Winfield and whoever destroyed that apartment is the same person."

"Alibis?"

"No one but Chartres has one for the time Lisa was attacked. Chartres's checks out, but when I saw him the other day, he had a strange look on his face."

"Strange how?"

"As if he knew something that I should know." Nash shook his head. "I don't know. Just a hunch."

"The background check on Chartres tell you anything new?"

"Nothing that I didn't already know. He was never busted for pimping. And he's been clean since. Until

I have hair matches, I'm not getting very far.'' He needed to know if the hairs were the same, female and matched Catherine Delan's.

''I'll see what I can do to hurry it up.''

Nash nodded and left the office. Suddenly Lisa's image tripped into his mind. Instinctively he reached for his cell phone, then stopped. Mainly because he didn't know what to say to her. Hell, he wasn't even sure what he was feeling other than anger and disappointment. He wasn't sure if it was in her or himself. He needed to get out of here, he thought, and was about to leave when an elderly man came into the station. He was nearly bald and had to be at least seventy-five, but his step was determined and fast. And headed right toward Nash.

''Detective Couviyon, I'm Councilman Gramarr,'' the man said, extending his hand.

Nash shook it, then frowned slightly. The name was familiar. ''You live next to the Baylor Inn.''

''Yes, for forty years. I remembered something about the night that young man was killed.''

Nash offered him a seat, his heartbeat picking up a bit. An officer called out, said he had a call from Chartres, and Nash waved him off to take a message. ''Go ahead, sir.''

''That night I was getting ready for bed. I usually close the shades and turn off most of the lights. I turned off all the lights except the bathroom. Left the windows open. There were guests of the inn on the patio, but they were not making any noise. Just before

I crawled into bed, I saw a shadow pass over my wall that night.''

Nash's hopes fell. This was too weak a lead.

"Now, son, I know what you're thinking, but I'm on my top floor, which is level with the inn, and I've lived in that house a long time. If the moon is up and someone's on the back staircase, it casts a shadow into my window. It's rare, mind you, and I didn't think much of it, because it happens when a good storm blows the trees. But this was different. I saw a figure.''

"Did this figure go in?''

"Well, the shadow disappeared, so I suspect so. But that's hard to tell, because once I close my eyes, I'm out.''

Baylor had insisted that none of his employees used the back stairs. "What time did you see this shadow?''

"It was after ten.''

"How's your eyesight, Mr. Gramarr?''

The older man's gaze pinned him. "To read the paper, terrible, but I can still sight a deer at fifty yards, boy.''

Nash smiled for the first time that day.

"I'm sorry this took so long, but like I said, I didn't think much of it till the other night when it happened again.''

"Again?''

"Yes, it was you walking up those steps.'' Gramarr stood to leave. "You haven't caught the killer, have you?''

"No, sir. But I will.''

At least he now knew how the killer had gotten inside Winfield's room. And though he couldn't prove it, he'd bet that gift basket was in the storage room on the second floor, delivered at six, then retrieved after Lisa left the suite. Chartres was an accomplice or had discovered it in the storage room and told no one. Nash tried calling Chartres at his home, but received no answer.

He tried a couple of more times without success, then went for ice cream. It seemed the sane thing to do. His brain was smoking from going over the facts of the case, and he didn't want to see Lisa right now. Being alone in a theater, a bar, or alone in his place didn't appeal to him right now. He was walking into the quaint little shop when someone grabbed his arm.

He turned sharply, his hand slipping inside his jacket for his weapon. A woman and a small boy stood near. "Laura?"

"Don't look so shocked, Nash," his former partner's widow said.

They hugged warmly. "I thought you'd moved," he said.

"No." Laura looked around. "This is home. I needed to be back here."

He smiled at Laura, stunned by how good she looked compared with the last time he'd seen her. "You look terrific. How are you doing?"

"Fine, keeping busy. Steven is a handful."

Nash looked down at the little boy, seeing his former partner in the child's small features. "Hey, pal."

"Hello, Officer Nash." The boy was tugging on his mother's hand, inching toward the door, clearly eager for an ice-cream cone and uninterested in the adults.

Nash held the door open. "My treat," he said, and Laura smiled and walked inside. Half an hour later, full of ice cream and sipping a soda, Nash marveled at the difference in Laura. Last time he'd seen her, a year after David's death, she'd been emotionally ruined and not getting better. David had left her financially stable for a few years, but that would never replace the loss of the man she loved.

Nash listened to her tell him what she'd been up to lately, listened to the little boy chatter, and he smiled. Steven was a three-foot package of energy and it hit Nash like a lightning bolt that if his and Lisa's child had survived, he or she would be about a year younger than Steven. At the same time he understood that Steven had never known his father, since he'd been an infant when David was killed.

The boy asked about his father, and Nash told him about David's heroism, about how he liked to fish even if he never caught anything. Nash felt Laura's smile, wondering if she was hurting still. When they left the shop, Steven skipped on ahead of them.

"I'm getting married again, Nash," Laura said.

His brows rose high. "I'm stunned."

"Are you happy for me?"

"Sure. You deserve it."

"I loved David, and I'll always miss him. Every time I look at Steven I see him. Joshua loves my son and me. He's been great with Steven." She stopped and looked up at Nash. "I've picked up the pieces and moved on."

"It was tough, wasn't it?"

"Yes. I won't kid you. I thought I'd never come back from the grief. But I had Steven. He needed me and that pulled me back." She smiled tenderly at the boy, who was frantically licking at the melting ice cream. "I had some great friends and family, but he made the difference. And there was you, too."

"I didn't do anything."

"You grieved with me, Nash, and that was enough." She tipped her head to the side. "So how's Lisa holding up?"

"You heard about her?"

She shook her head, amused. "I had lunch with her a couple of weeks before Peter was killed."

Nash's eyes flared and for a second he just stared at her. "God. I've had my head in the dirt, haven't I?"

Laura smiled softly. "I don't know about that, but when David was killed, a lot of the officers' wives drifted away. Lisa never abandoned me, Nash, even after you two broke up. She brought meals over. She cared for Steven so I could rest. We've kept in touch over the past few years."

This was news to him. "She never told me."

"I'm not surprised."

"Why?" He felt the arrow coming before it found the target.

"She loved you, Nash, but she took a stand because she needed to for her own peace. She would never have told you about the baby because she knew you'd do the right thing and resent her for trapping you. Why should she give you any more of herself now? She already did that once, and you didn't even fight for her."

That arrow hit dead center, piercing his heart and nearly bringing him to his knees. Four years ago, he'd loved Lisa and was too caught up in himself to recognize it till it was too late. A second chance loomed, and this time he was smarter.

Chapter Ten

The next morning, Nash stared at the dead body of John Chartres. Slumped in an easy chair, the man looked nothing as he had at the inn. His crisp suit and tie was replaced with jeans and a ratty T-shirt. But it was the trash-filled studio apartment decorated with too much red satin and a half-dozen velvet Elvis portraits that spoke loudly. Nash could almost smile. What a fake, Nash thought. But as Quinn Kilpatrick snapped off the latex gloves and walked toward Nash, all amusement dissolved. Nash was the victim's only voice.

"Let me guess. Poisoned?" Nash asked, gesturing to the cup on its side on the floor.

"Yes, pennyroyal tea. I'm guessing right now."

Lisa had told Nash that pennyroyal was often mistaken for a mint and was toxic. "So don't quote you?" Nash said.

"Yes, I'd bet there was more in that cup than herbs. Smells like arsenic."

Good God. "Someone's eliminating the suspects,"

Nash said aloud, and as he did, panic gripped him. If suspects were dying, then Lisa was in trouble. And when Nash left the scene he hoped he could get to her in time.

LISA STROLLED barefoot through her garden, locking the back gate for the night. Last evening she and Hope had progressed from ice cream to wine and ended with both of them falling asleep and wishing they hadn't partied quite so enthusiastically. Lisa woke to a funny note from Hope and the place cleaned up, but her day didn't get any better.

If she wanted Nash, would she have to go after him? Would she be the one fighting for more and finding nothing? Hope's advice sounded logical after a couple glasses of chardonnay, but now, well, it made Lisa fear she'd come across as pitiful and needy. And she wasn't. She'd managed just fine for a long time without Nash.

Have you really? a voice in her head asked, much to her annoyance. She knew Nash was wondering why she really married Peter and didn't believe the pat, ''I loved him and he loved me there for a while'' answer. The truth was, she'd gone to Peter because she'd waited for Nash to come to her, and when he hadn't, she'd given up. It was the hardest thing in the world to do, giving up, and when she'd mistakenly called Peter by Nash's name a couple of times, it only showed that her subconscious was working against her. And Peter never let her forget those slips, either.

Lisa strolled the stone path back toward the house, pausing to gaze at her shop and home and feel the warmth of pride. Tension melted from her at the sight of it all, softly lit, Spanish moss swaying like lace in the dark. Most people would think that looked creepy, but the gnarled, spreading oaks and moss reminded her she was home, even if her parents were living the retired life in Florida.

She mounted the steps to the shop section on the west side of the house and locked up behind herself before stepping into the mudroom that connected the business to her home. Suddenly unable to recall if she'd secured the shop's front door after Kate and Chris had left, Lisa backtracked through the shop. She hadn't locked it, so she did now, noticing the patrol car sitting across the street. Nash's extra pair of eyes, she thought, and the image of the butcher knife plunged into her nightgown made her shiver. She didn't know who hated her that much. Catherine Delan had Peter in more ways than in his bed. What would she gain from hurting Lisa now?

Walking back into the house, intent on setting the electronic alarm once she was inside, she'd just stepped into the mudroom when the outside lights went off.

"Damn." She moved to the switchplate in the back of the shop, instinctively shifting around pots and display crates. Then a creak split the silence. She stilled and scanned the darkened area. "Who's there?"

Chris and Kate had gone home more than two hours

ago. Really ticked off that she was scared in her own home, Lisa marched toward the back of the shop where clay and ceramic pots lined a display shelf with seed packets and small gardening tools. She'd reached the end of the shelf where the breaker switches were when someone grabbed her by the throat and yanked.

NASH CALLED IN for backup as he turned into Lisa's driveway. Rushing to the front door, he found it locked, the floodlights out. He raced to the side of the house where the shop was located, heard scuffling, and as sirens blasted the night behind him, Nash called out to Lisa, shoving his shoulder against the door.

The lock fractured, the door slapping back against the wall. He saw Lisa on her knees, gasping for breath.

"Oh, God." He reached for her.

She smacked away his hands. "They went out the side. Damn them, they broke my greenhouse door."

Nash raced to the west side and out the door, then jumped over the three steps down before thrashing through the yard toward the back gate in time to catch the vibrating of the back fence. Someone had jumped it, he thought, and in the pitch-black, he threw himself over the wood rail and dropped to the ground. Weapon out, Nash scanned the area, listening, then he heard it. Footsteps, a steady thump. He ran, radioing in his location. Officers arrived and spread out, a car moving down the next street. Mounted search lamps swept the area, smooth against the flashing blue cruiser lights.

"Somebody talk to me," he growled into the radio

as he ran. He cleared a chain-link fence, then rounded a house, following the sounds of the footsteps for two blocks.

"Pond Road is clear. Nothing here, sir," came back over the radio, and two other officers broke in to tell him they'd found nothing and where they were headed next.

Nash kept running, sliding into a rain ditch, then sprinting into the street again. "I'm east, on Magnolia."

Nothing. The street was empty and half the streetlights were out. Nash cursed, moving forward still, his gaze shifting over the ground, the fences. Houses lined the streets and doors were closed. A couple of citizens peered out into the dark, and Nash knew that none of them could see clearly. These homes were old, mostly without garages. There were few places to hide.

Though he knew it was probably useless, he called in for officers to canvas the next three streets in all directions and block the area off.

"Do we have a description of the suspect?" an officer asked.

"No, we don't." But maybe Lisa had seen something.

Nash hadn't seen more than a shadow in the darkness. The lights around Lisa's place had been out. Cursing under his breath, he headed back to the house.

She was in her living room, a half-dozen cops in her shop and house. Sitting on the sofa, her arms wrapped across her middle, she rocked.

Nash knelt in front of her. "Lisa?"

She looked up. Her eyes were blazing with fury. "You find this person, Nash, before I do something really mean like keep a gun."

"Calm down, honey." Hell, he wanted to find whoever had done this and beat the hell out of him. Or her. But Nash had to keep Lisa calm so she could think clearly and just maybe give him enough to catch whoever had hurt her.

She stood, glaring at him as he rose to his full height. "Calm? This is my house! My home! They broke in and tried to kill me!"

Her voice was hoarse and his gaze lowered to the red marks on her throat. Ignoring her fury, he touched the marks. "I know, I know. How do you feel?"

She pushed his hand away. "I'm fine." She cleared her throat. "Hey," she snapped at an officer. "Wipe your feet before you step on that rug."

Nash smothered a smile and sent the officers outside. A team was already dusting for prints.

"Don't bother, they were wearing gloves," Lisa said to them.

"You keep saying 'they.' Was there more than one person?" Nash asked.

"No."

"Did you see anything?"

"No, I didn't see anything. They came from behind, *again!*" Her voice rang with disgust and just a trace of the fear that must still be crawling through her. "I hit whoever it was in the stomach with my elbow, but that didn't do much.''

"It was enough to get away.''

She met his gaze, not seeing her advantage right now. "No, they were going to town on my throat when you drove up. They just let go and ran.'' Lisa pushed her way between uniformed cops and into her shop. She groaned miserably. Though the outside greenhouse door was shattered, the door leading from there into the house was intact. But the lock was gone, taken right out. She started searching for it, without any luck.

"The connections to the lights were cut, sir,'' an officer said, coming inside. "The register is untouched.''

Nash looked at Lisa and ran his hand over her arm. The action was soothing, like a tranquilizer to her raw nerve endings. "Did you set the alarms?''

"I hadn't had the chance,'' she said, scooping one hand back through her hair in a tired gesture. "I was just locking up and shutting off the water system.''

"Was the greenhouse locked?''

"Always. Both doors. Customers have a tendency to wander in there if I don't.''

"Who has a key?'' Nash asked.

"What does it matter? They didn't use it!''

"Lisa.''

"Me. Only I have one.''

"Not your employees?''

"No. It's my sanctuary and I don't let too many people in there."

His lips curved a fraction and his gaze warmed her. Lisa wanted badly to fall into his arms and let his strength smooth the ruffles between them. But just the same, she was angry that it had taken a killer to bring him to her.

"The inside alarm is intact, but not the one in the shop," an officer said.

Lisa looked around, her expression crushed.

"I can board up the doors till tomorrow," Nash offered, dialing his brother's number. "But you should empty the shop of anything you can't replace."

Lisa shook her head. "It's all insured. I'll put the register inside, though. I'm going to make some coffee," she said glumly, heading for the kitchen.

Nash watched her go, tamping down his rage over this and then speaking hurriedly with his brother.

By the time Lisa came back with a carafe of coffee and a fistful of mugs, Temple had arrived. And looking too good for his own self this late at night, Lisa thought, doling out mugs of coffee. With help from a couple of officers they boarded the broken door.

"Ma'am," an officer said, tipping his hat as they collected up her tools and replaced them in the box.

"You didn't have to do that," she said to Nash.

"Yeah, I did," Nash said, putting the toolbox back in the storeroom. "Temple," Nash said, and his sibling moved up beside Lisa. The brothers exchanged a look she couldn't decipher.

"Lisa, I want you to come with me for the night," Nash said quietly, his gaze locking with hers.

The thought of being anywhere alone with Nash right now sounded at once comforting and scary. "Where? Your place?" She frowned at the two men.

"Indigo Run," Nash said.

"Don't fight us on this, Lisa," Temple added. "We can protect you there."

"I don't think that's necessar—"

"John Chartres is dead," Nash told Lisa. "Poisoned."

Lisa swallowed hard and nodded. "Let me get a few things together."

AS NASH DROVE UP the long, oak-lined drive, it was as if Lisa had stepped back three centuries. Indigo Run Plantation took her breath away, each tree along the drive silhouetted against the darkness with lights at the base. The house alone was enough to make any woman's mouth water. All that space. With double balconies facing the drive and wrapping the lower floor, the house was rambling and white with a carriage house and outer buildings. The Charleston green shutters looked black in the darkness.

As they stopped before the house, a tall man stepped out onto the porch, the polished oak door gleaming behind him and reflecting light from inside.

Nash opened the car door for her, and Lisa stepped out, her gaze shifting around the area. "I bet it's terrific in the daylight," she said, her voice gravelly.

Nash's fist tightened on the car doorframe and he tried to shrug. But inside he was ashamed of himself for not letting her into this part of his life before. "It's home."

She met his gaze. "It's *your* home."

"No, Lisa—" he moved closer "—this is where I grew up. I live downtown. You know that."

Was he trying to apologize for not bringing her here? Well, she'd rather he didn't. "Oh, for pity's sake, Nash, stop splitting hairs," she said, and walked up the wide Federal steps.

Nash shook his head and took her bag from the trunk.

"Hello, Logan."

"Miss Lisa Bracket," he said, his voice deep and holding a wealth of emotion. "It's about time my brother smartened up."

"He didn't," she threw back. "Someone tried to kill me tonight."

Logan's body went perfectly still, his dark gaze snapping to his younger brother. "Is this true? Temple said there was trouble, not attempted murder."

"Yes, its true. And I'm getting smarter," Nash groused from behind her. "Come on, let's get inside before the gnats eat me alive."

Lisa walked inside with Logan, ignoring Nash, and stopped in the foyer.

"My, my," was all she could say. Deep pecan wooden walls shone with three hundred years of tender care, the foyer and hall were peppered with antiques and paintings and the biggest curved staircase she'd ever seen twisted up to the next floor. She was in awe that this place was still standing and imagined all the Couviyons who'd come before.

Logan moved close and said softly, "You're most welcome here, Lisa. Make yourself at home, you hear?"

She smiled up at the oldest Couviyon brother. "Thank you, Logan."

One brother was missing, Hunter, a CIA agent off protecting the country.

A woman, reed slim and gray-haired, emerged from the far end of the hall, moving quickly toward her. "I'm MaryGrace." She held out her hand. "And though Mr. Logan likes to think hisself in charge, I really am." Logan rocked on his heels and barely smiled. "So if you want anything a'tall, you just holler. Wait around for a man to get a clue and you'll likely grow cobwebs."

Lisa smiled.

"Come on, let's get you some supper," MaryGrace said, hustling Lisa down the hall. "Mr. Nash, you put her bag upstairs in the yellow room. And be quick; I've got dumplings I can't leave for a second."

"Yes, ma'am," he said, smiling as the two women went off toward the kitchen. He heard MaryGrace tell Lisa she needed to put some ice on her wound, and she'd fix her some horehound tea for her throat.

It hit Nash all over again that Lisa could have died tonight, and an icy chill spilled down his spine. He'd

be lost without her. Dying inside again. He lifted
Lisa's single bag and headed toward the staircase.

"Nash," Logan called.

Poised on the stairs, he turned, meeting his brother's
gaze and waiting. If Logan had something to say, he
took his time saying it.

Logan rocked back on his heels. "She's wonderful
and you're a fool."

"Yes, I know. Thank you for pointing that out yet
again." A man could always count on family to tell it
like it was. At least in this family that was true.

"Do you think she'll give you a second chance?"

"I don't see where it's any business of yours, Logan."

"She'll be safe here," Logan said, as if saying it
made it so.

"That's why she's here."

"I think you need to ask yourself why she's really
here again, little brother," Logan murmured before
walking into the study and closing the door.

Nash stared up at the ceiling for a second, knowing
he was going to get it from all sides tonight, then
ascended the stairs. Not like he didn't deserve it, he
thought.

"I DON'T NEED help, Miss Lisa. I've been doing this
for near on forty years now."

"I know, MaryGrace, but just let me do something." Lisa picked up a dish towel and dried a piece
of crystal.

MaryGrace eyed her. "Three Couviyon brothers are a bit much in one dose?"

Lisa moaned. "Yes, ma'am. One is plenty."

"Mr. Nash hasn't been the same without you, darlin'," the housekeeper said softly.

"He managed well enough."

MaryGrace shook her head, pushing Lisa into a chair and handing her another cup of lemon-and-horehound tea. Respectfully sipping, Lisa swore she was going to float away.

"The night you married that man, he came here, drunk and angry and wanting to rent a helicopter to go to New York and get you." MaryGrace shook her head at the memory.

Lisa met her gaze, her heart thundering. "But he didn't."

"Can't say as I know why, either."

"I do." It would have been committing himself to her. He would have had to actually love her. Lost chances and yesterdays, she thought, and wondered when the past would stop haunting them.

"You two talking about me?"

Lisa twisted on the stool as Nash stepped into the room.

"Of course," MaryGrace said, drying a pan. "And if you wanted to hear the good stuff, you should have lingered outside the door."

Nash grinned.

"Are you three done hashing over my situation?"

Lisa asked, inclining her head toward the dining room, where Temple and Logan were.

"It's more than a situation, Lisa. Someone tried to kill you tonight."

"Yes, they did. But because you arrived, they didn't. Did I thank you for that?"

He didn't smile, his gaze lowering to the marks on her throat. "Thank me when I find them."

Lisa's spine stiffened. Couldn't he just accept her thanks? "Good night, all," she said, glancing at Logan and Temple coming in behind him. "Thank you, MaryGrace. I appreciate you staying up so late and feeding me."

Nash was about to tell Lisa that dinner was usually late at Indigo Run, but she was already headed out of the kitchen.

Nash blinked. "Now what did I do?"

MaryGrace sent Nash a tired look. "You haven't grown a brain in the last four years. Don't know why I 'spect you had."

"She wanted to thank her hero and you trashed that," Temple said into the quiet, leaning back against the counter, his thumbs hooked in his jean pockets.

Nash looked at Logan. "You have criticism to offer, too?"

"I'm sure I could add to it, but I'm guessing she's got it in her head to leave. I suggest you get upstairs before she manages it. It'll be open season on her if she does."

Before his brother finished, Nash was storming

through the house to the stairs and mounting them two at a time. He didn't bother to knock and pushed open the guest-room door.

Wrapped in a blue silk robe, Lisa was sitting on the edge of the bed, and she looked up as he entered.

"You're not going anywhere," he said, crossing to her and lifting her by the arms from the bed.

"Really?" She wasn't planning on leaving.

"You're staying right here till I find the person who hurt you."

Was that his only reason for bringing her here? "Am I?"

"Yes, dammit."

"And how long will that take? I've got a business to run."

"Close it."

"No. That will be like knuckling under."

Frustrated fury exploded in his features. "It will be like keeping you alive! I'll help you if you lose money."

"I don't want your help."

"Why are you being like this?"

She pushed out of his arms. "Why are you so hell-bent on putting me under glass when you stormed out of my house three days ago and haven't said a word to me since!" She put space between them and knew it wasn't enough.

Nash plowed his fingers through his hair and let out a long-suffering breath. "Good grief, Lisa. I'm not doing this very well, am I?"

"Doing what?"

"Apologizing."

She didn't utter a sound for a long moment. "For what?"

"For not protecting you when I said I would. For not being there when you needed me. For not fighting for you when it was all I wanted to do then."

Lisa blinked. "Well, that's a mouthful."

He met her gaze. "I didn't want my job to leave you like David's death left Laura."

"Oh, Nash, you can't live on maybes, and your job never mattered to me. I didn't fall in love with a cop. I fell in love with you."

The hope leaping through his heart about killed him right then.

"I'm fine and Laura's fine," Lisa said.

"I know. I saw her and little Steven."

"She looks good, doesn't she? And her fiancé is a terrific guy."

Nash's gaze locked with hers. "You didn't break a single tie to Indigo when you married Winfield, did you."

"Except the one with you."

"That's not your fault, it's mine. No, don't try to soften it," he said when she opened her mouth to argue. "I thought you'd always be there and it never occurred to me that you wouldn't be." He sat on the dainty yellow sofa beneath the window, his elbows on his knees, his gaze on his clasped hands.

He looked hopelessly out of place in the delicate room, Lisa thought, her blood running like quicksilver through her veins. Whatever he had to say, though, she needed to hear it.

"I was destroyed when you left. I blamed you for wanting too much from me, I blamed you for leaving with the next guy who came along…" He met her gaze, his expression full of self-recrimination. "I know, I know, it was a while before Winfield showed up, but not to me. I'd lost everyone who'd meant anything to me, and you were the one person I needed." He rubbed his mouth. "And then you were out of my reach."

"You didn't bother to reach for me and I waited as long as I could. Then, after losing the baby—" her voice quavered "—I gave up. I couldn't take it anymore. I loved you and you didn't want me."

His eyes flashed with denial. "That's not true."

"You wanted me sometimes, Nash, but only when you chose to let me in the private circle you kept so tight around yourself. I understand. I swear I do. But you should have turned to me. I was the only one who gave a damn!"

When he just stared, she headed for her suitcase. She'd thought she wanted to hear all this. But she'd changed her mind. Rehashing the past was just resurrecting the pain. "I can't do this anymore."

He darted across the room, latching on to her arm and turning her to face him. "Don't leave me again."

Her heart crumbled and she searched his blue eyes, feeling herself fall deep into him.

Nash closed his arms around her, afraid for the first time in his life. "Don't go. Not because your life's in danger, but because mine is." He stroked her hair back off her face. "I know I didn't give you much choice back then, but…" He was quiet for a second, his gaze roaming over her face. "Stay, Lisa. I'm in love with you. And without you, my life is empty."

Tears filled her eyes and her lip quivered.

"I was in love with you four years ago, too, but I thought loving you would only bring you pain, like it did Laura. I wasn't being noble—I was being selfish. To both of us, because my feelings are still here." He cupped her jaw, gazing deeply into her eyes. "It might have been hidden under other feelings, but the minute I saw you again, I knew nothing inside me had changed. I love you."

She pushed his hair off his brow, trailing her fingers down the side of his face. "I've waited so long to hear that." A tear plumped and rolled down her cheek.

"Has it been too long?" His expression, his very tone, was stripped of pride, his heart laid bare for her to gather close. Or release him now.

Lisa swallowed, fighting tears. "No, not too long." She felt his muscles give only a fraction, tension still locking her in his arms.

"Is there a chance you still love me?"

She smiled, tears falling. "Oh, yeah, there's a good chance."

Chapter Eleven

"Yeah?" His smile widened.

"I love you, Nash."

For a second he closed his eyes and thanked God that he got what he didn't really deserve. He met her gaze, dropping a soft kiss on her lips.

"I've never stopped," she said. "I just tucked it away, pushed it aside. I married Peter, hoping he would get you out of my heart."

"The more I learned about him, the more I wondered why you married him." Nash ran his hand over her hair and down her spine, sending shivers of warmth over her skin.

"Now you know." She draped her arms across his shoulders. "He wasn't you."

Nash hated to think of all these years gone. The time spent apart when they could have been together. And he had only himself to blame. "I wish I'd been smarter. I've wasted so much time."

"Let's not waste any more time, okay? In fact, you

can start making up for some of it by kissing me right now.''

''Oh, yeah?''

She pushed her fingers into his hair, cupping the back of his head and drawing him down. ''You know—'' she brushed his mouth with hers, teasing him ''—if being this slow on the uptake is going to be a problem in the future, Couviyon,'' she said against his lips, ''we need to fix that.''

His hands made a wild ride over her body.

''I'll see what I can do.'' His mouth covered hers and Lisa's world suddenly bloomed with heat, his warm kiss filled with a fresh beginning, repairing the gouges in her heart. It wasn't like before, no old memories clouded, except his warmth and power. Nash might be a modern-day lawman, but his kisses were old-fashioned slow, deep and sultry. Torturing to her senses, making her toes curl in her shoes, her heart thump so hard she was sure it would choke her.

He deepened his kiss, his breathing hurried like hers, and when she moaned with pleasure, Nash felt his knees start to give way and he clutched her tighter. He wanted to claim her. Now. He wanted it all, to marry her, make babies with her—everything he'd walked away from. And the patience that made him a good cop failed him right now.

''Nash,'' she murmured. ''I've missed you.''

''I've missed you, too, baby.'' He slid his hand up from her waist, covering her breast, and she pushed into him, tugging his shirt free, shoving her hands beneath the fabric and stroking his warm, hard muscles.

They touched, palms searching for skin, for pleasure, their kiss unending, a dark surrender and a plea for more.

"Nash, touch me. Please." Lisa undid the buttons of his shirt. "It's been so long." She pushed her hands inside, stroking his skin and setting him on fire. Beneath her nightgown, he found her, bare and warm, and he enfolded her breasts, gently circling her nipples into tight peaks.

She tried smothering her moans.

"I want to hear you," he said, moving his hand lower, nudging her thighs apart.

"This house is filled with people."

"The walls are thick, trust me."

She gazed into his eyes, seeing determination and desire. It made her hotter.

"Open for me, baby."

She did and he easily slid a finger inside her. "Oh, Nash." Her pulse shot up another ten notches.

He stroked her softness, watching her face, committing it to memory. After a moment or two, instinct took over, her hips rocking, and she pulled at the satin straps and exposed her breast. Nash didn't need any more invitation and laid her back on the cushions, taking her nipple deep into his mouth.

Lisa felt her world focus on his mouth toying with her nipple. Nash had incredible patience and stamina.

And four years hadn't made a wit of difference. The man could play for hours.

And he did.

He tasted her flesh, his stroking fingers bringing her passion higher and higher. At every shift and thrust, Lisa felt the seams inside her rip with sensation. She clung harder, rocked faster and fought through the haze to reach his belt buckle. "Inside me. Please, I want you inside me."

He shook his head and kept stroking her, knowing what she liked, knowing she was on the edge. He wanted to see the tumble. "Take this, baby. Let me watch it."

Her gaze locked with his as pleasure raced over her skin, hummed inside her, trying to get out. Nash absorbed it, could almost taste it as her body clenched him, and when she bowed, he experienced the luscious, untamed waves as they poured through her.

As the haze softened, he waited for her breathing to slow, then kissed her softly.

"That was a bit more vocal than I remember," he murmured, worrying her lips.

"I screamed, didn't I?"

He grinned. "Oh, yeah."

She buried her face in his shoulder, praying she hadn't woken the household. That was not the impression she wanted Logan, Temple or MaryGrace to have of her. "I think you should go to your room." It was her only hope, if he left, because she wanted him naked on the floor right now.

"Not a chance."

"I'm not doing anything with you unless you gag me."

"I can fix that."

He scooped her up in his arms and stood, then left the room.

"Nash, put me down," she whispered against his neck, praying no one discovered them.

"No. I want to make love to you."

Her insides jumped at that. "I'd hoped so."

"And I want privacy."

"In this house?"

He kept walking down the long hall, passing door after door and then bent to open the last one. "This was my room."

He stepped inside and set her on her feet.

Lisa stared. "Oh, dear, you grew up in this room?"

He shut the door. "Yeah. Frightening huh?"

Lisa's gaze traveled over the green walls trimmed in white, the massive, and she did mean massive, four-poster rice bed that reached to the ceiling. A paddle fan made a lazy turn, stirring the heavy green brocade drapes. "It's lovely but—"

"Not the room you imagine a teenager in, huh?"

"No." It was perfect for a man, not a teenager. It was another part of his past she hadn't understood.

"Well, I rarely got to be one. I'm a Couviyon and upholding family traditions was more important than doing what I wanted."

"I hear years of resentment."

"Just a little, yeah. I didn't get to skip school or hang out with my friends. I volunteered at homeless shelters, played ball for prep schools like my brothers, and attended cotillion balls because my parents' friends wanted dates for their daughters."

"So that's where you learned to dance so well."

He nodded, turning on only one small lamp but opening the drapes to let moonlight stream into the room. She noticed trophies in barrister bookcases and a few framed pictures and awards, but all were made part of the decor. The room was gigantic.

He toed off his shoes, yanked at his socks.

Lisa smiled and slid her robe off her shoulders, giving Nash a full view of the short blue satin nightgown. The sight of her standing there, wanting him, loving him after all the heartache, hit him like a train. In one night he'd nearly lost her and then he'd regained her love. He was a lucky man, and he wasn't about to forget that. Not ever. He walked toward her.

"Why did we come here?"

"It's far enough away from the other rooms that no one will here us."

"No one?"

He shook his head.

"Does that bed creak?"

He grinned. "A little."

"Then I won't be the only one making noise." Lisa pushed the straps of her nightgown off her shoulders and wiggled, letting the satin nightie fall and pool at her feet without a sound.

Nash swallowed visibly. Then he stripped, moving toward her, pausing once to kick aside his trousers. Lisa leaned back against the bedpost, smiling and enjoying his approach. Seeing how prepared he was for her, made her power sing through her veins.

Then he was against her, pressing his body to hers, his hands skating over her body. His kiss was deep and wrapped in emotions. Lisa let them coat her, feeling his heart pound against hers, and thought, *I would have waited a lifetime to love this man again.*

She felt electrified. Nash was trembling.

"I want you so much," he murmured against her mouth, his skin on fire from her touch. And man, was she touching. Her fingers wrapped his arousal, and Nash groaned, wanting to push into her now, end this torment just so they could start again.

She stroked him, and they were a tangle of rushing fingers and thick kisses. Nash couldn't take it, and he pried her free, sliding his hand up her body and pushing her arms around the bedpost.

"I have this fantasy," he said, and she arched a brow.

"Fulfill it," she said, and the trust between them strengthened.

Nash kissed her mouth, the tips of her breasts, his tongue rasping over her skin and leaving her damp and hungry. His teeth scraped the underside of her breast on a path downward, his hands unmoving on her hips.

Only his lips and tongue touched her, and it was so erotic she couldn't help watching. He moved lower and anticipation skated sharply through her. Her blood heated as he licked her hip, then her thigh. On his knees, he slid his hands around her behind, then hooked one of her knees and lifted it onto his shoulder.

Then he feasted.

Lisa cried out his name, aching from the post, and struggling to remain standing when everything in her said fall. He plunged his tongue deeply, and she sank her fingers into his hair, watching him, wanting to do the same for him and feel him break like glass for her. Lisa's stomach clenched, her hips curling.

"Nash, please. I want you."

He kept playing.

"Nash!"

He stood, lifting her off her feet, and she wrapped her legs around him.

"Now!" she gasped. "Oh, please. Now."

Smiling, Nash laid her onto the bed, her body cradling him and she reached between them, sliding the tip of him against her slick opening.

He slammed his eyes shut, then, braced above her, he pushed, loving her squirming, her impatience. He filled her, his gaze locked with hers as he withdrew and plunged deeply again.

Nash laced his fingers with hers as he thrust and withdrew, setting a cadence that clawed at her nerves, taunted her desire. Lisa took him in like a fine wine she'd been denied, with a thirst that quenched her soul. Muscles rippled as he trembled, his breath a shiver of pleasure against her lips. His hips moved like warm honey, long, slow undulations that drove her mad. And drove deeper.

She pulsed, with life, with love. It was tangible between them. A song in her blood, the words on her lips.

"I love you," he said, and kept moving, a little faster, a little harder.

She chanted his name in a demand, her hips rising to greet him. Nash fought his control and whispered that he loved her, loved that righteous look she got when she was defensive, that she was the only woman who made him feel vulnerable, and he cherished that. He murmured that he loved the taste of her, loved the way she clamped him so tightly he could feel her blood pulsing. He'd never forgotten—years of dreams had tormented him—wanting her, having her like this. Yet when she was gone, in another man's arms, it had destroyed what was left in him. It seeded anger, and as he made love to her, filled her, that anger seeped away, like a tide bringing back new feelings, new sensations, fresh and greedy.

Lisa searched his face, feeling tears spill and roll into her hair. Here in the dark, he was saying what she'd longed to hear. That he couldn't live without her. Neither could she.

"Finish me," he said, and when he ground against her center, she gripped his hips, pulling him harder into her. His control snapped.

He rushed into her, and Lisa arched off the bed, crazy with desire. "Oh, mercy," she whispered, and touched his face, his throat, and Nash clutched her to him, the eruption shattering through him with a shudder that threatened his composure.

They clung, a tangle of limbs on the ancient bed, hearts reborn as they fell over the edge of rapture and into their own slice of heaven.

Chapter Twelve

Hours later Lisa stirred, tucked in the comfort of Nash's arms. She felt safe and loved. Oh, Lord, had she been well loved last night! All over the room and even out on the balcony under the stars. When she shifted, he closed his arms more tightly around her.

"Stay."

"I need to go back to my room."

"Nah." He nuzzled her neck, rising up a bit to find more skin to taste. His lips closed over her tender nipple, and sheer pleasure shimmered though her.

"Nash…honey…oh, that feels good, but Mary-Grace will be awake soon, and I'd like to keep my reputation with her."

"Believe me, MaryGrace will know you were here. Nothing gets past that woman." He shifted over Lisa, nudging her thighs apart.

"All the more reason to go…" He slid smoothly into her, her body awake and primed in seconds. "Oh, Nash."

He arched a brow, smiling. "Reason enough to

stay?'' he murmured, thrusting into her in that slow gentle way that drove her crazy.

Mouths met and melted, her body capturing his, and drawing him back into her. "I think so."

He pushed harder, a little faster. Slick, and steamy with heat.

"Oh, yeah," she said on a laugh. "I see the light."

"I want you to see stars."

He pumped into her, loving her awake, and before the sun rose, Nash showered her with stars.

NASH STEPPED into the kitchen, expecting to find Lisa, but the room was empty. Frowning, he started searching the house. She'd slipped out before dawn. She didn't want anyone seeing her leaving his room. He didn't blame her. In a house like this, there were some rules you stuck to, even if you bent them a little during the night.

A needle of panic pricked his spine when he didn't find her. He was in the back of the house, walking toward the solarium, when he heard her voice. He passed through the double doors, stopping when he saw the change in the solarium. A week ago it had showed its neglect with dead flowers and drying trees, leaves scattering the tile floors. Now it was clean, the dead plants gone, the floor gleaming.

He heard laughter and then through the open doors he saw her out on the back porch. Walking through the solarium and out into the sun, he stopped short.

His gaze snapped from Lisa, then to his mother.

The pair were bent over a rosebush, pruning it. Both women wore gloves, and while his mother wore a straw hat and dress, Lisa had on shorts and a T-shirt. And she was barefoot.

"Hello, Nash," Lisa said, turning toward him and meeting his gaze.

She gave him a sexy smile, and for a moment last night played in his mind with enough clarity to make him hard. Lisa gripping the headboard as he pushed into her, making love to her again on his balcony under the stars, the raw power in her, and he understood the big difference between having sex and making love. She'd taught him most of the night till they fell into his bed, drained and satisfied. He was ready right now to drag her upstairs and do it all over again.

She left his mother, walked nearer. His mom kept clipping roses.

"You shouldn't look at me like that in public," she said.

He smiled, then brushed her mouth with his. His mother looked at them blankly, then went back to cutting blooms.

Nash pulled back and rubbed Lisa's arm. "I'm sorry you had to see her like this."

"Don't be sorry. I understand. I found her wandering around alone this morning." She glanced back at the older woman. "We're becoming good friends."

As the only witness to her husband's murder, Olivia Couviyon was trapped in the fog that had claimed her mind the night Nash's father died. The loving mother

Nash and his brothers had grown up with had disappeared, replaced with a fragile woman who wandered listlessly around Indigo Run. None of them knew if she was aware that her husband was dead, because she never spoke of their father or that night. And the doctors wouldn't let them question her. They were afraid if forced, Olivia Couviyon would never come back.

"Why didn't you tell me?" Lisa asked Nash.

"There's nothing anyone can do. And I don't think anything will change till we learn who killed my father and why."

Lisa nodded and sympathized. Olivia Couviyon had been a town matriarch. The rumors that she'd gone crazy after her husband's death weren't pretty. But Lisa had found a gentle woman locked in a different time. Smart, witty, but not crazy.

"The solarium used to be her favorite place," Nash said.

"She wouldn't come inside."

"She won't come inside the house at all, Lisa. She lives in the cottage out back. She ignores Logan, looks right through him, and talks to me and my brothers like we're still in college."

"To her, I think you are."

He frowned.

"She's trapped somewhere where there isn't any pain, Nash. I met your father, seen pictures of him. Logan looks so much like Sebastian when he was younger its uncanny. So for your mom to acknowledge Logan would be accepting your father is dead."

"That's what the doctors think." Nash did, too.

"Didn't she witness his murder?"

"We think so. My father was dead, and we found her wandering outside the house."

"There's not a chance she might have…"

"Killed him?"

If Lisa expected anger, she didn't get it.

"I've thought of that. I'm the only one willing to consider that possibility. But they loved each other and she didn't have an angry bone in her body. She never once raised her voice at us when we were kids."

"Lisa, dear."

Lisa turned toward Olivia. "Yes, ma'am."

"You come with me and let Nash get on with his studies."

Nash sent Lisa a look that said, *See what I mean?*

Lisa took a step toward Olivia, but Nash pulled her back into his arms. He kissed her and Lisa responded, falling under his spell.

"I missed you this morning," he said softly, rubbing her spine.

She smiled. "I plan on sneaking into your room tonight, so don't go locking your door."

"I'm smarter than that."

"Yeah, *now*."

He stroked her hair off her face, his expression troubled.

"What's the matter?" Lisa asked.

She read him too well. "Not a damn thing catching

a killer won't solve." And a few other things, he thought. "Promise me you'll stay here today?"

"I promise. I have plenty to keep me occupied." She gestured at the solarium.

"That's great, but no going back to your place. Not even for plants."

She nodded, touching her throat. The red marks were still visible, and Nash tipped her chin, staring at them like a cop. Small hands, he thought.

"Lisa, dear, don't dally," his mother called. She'd moved farther away.

"I have to go. She needs me."

His heart broke open and flooded with love for her. How did he get so damn lucky? "I'll see you at lunch."

Lisa nodded, pushing out of his arms when she wanted to stay right there. "Will you go by Kate's place and tell her the store is closed? I couldn't get her on the phone."

"Sure." He kissed her. "I love you," he said, and he thought her eyes teared up a bit. Yet she mouthed the same words back, then headed toward his mother.

Nash watched her for a moment, the two women hovering over a rosebush. His heart, where his mother was concerned, just got a little lighter.

NASH WAS GRABBING a cup of coffee at the Daily Grind before work when Hope Randall came up beside him. She nudged him with her elbow.

"Well, as I live and breathe, it's Detective Couvi-yon."

"Hello, Hope." His gaze slid over her, noticing the deep tan, and her hair streaked from the sun. "Your vacation agrees with you. Sad to be back?"

"Oh, gee, let's see... Sun, surf, room service, mus-cled cabana boys at my beck and call, or peeping into people's private lives and sifting through their gar-bage. Tough choice."

He laughed. "I hear you." Right now Nash could use a week off, too, as long as it was with Lisa.

"I saw Lisa," Hope said.

"So did I, this morning."

She arched a brow and turned serious. "I love her like a sister, and you'd best be making wedding plans. I'd hate to have to hurt you."

Nash chuckled. Hope was a petite brunette with more energy than five women. She was a martial-arts expert, not to mention an excellent shot with a gun. Add the mouth that roared and that she'd been a cop for a short time, and Hope Randall was a powerhouse to be reckoned with. "And I don't doubt you could, Randall."

They paid for their coffees and moved away from the counter. He told Hope about the attack and that Lisa was at Indigo Run.

"About time."

"God, are you going to harass me, too, for my stu-pidity?"

"That you are man enough to admit it is a step in

the right direction. But considering I didn't say a word when you *were* being a jerk, I figure I've got some good digs coming to me. I want to savor them.'' She licked the whipped cream off her latte.

"I love her," Nash blurted.

Hope grinned.

"I want to marry her."

Her face brightened further. "Okay, you just got into my 'guys with white hats' club."

Nash laughed.

"What club is that?" a voice said, and they turned as Temple strolled up. Nash could feel the sudden animosity radiating from Hope like a wire about to snap.

"None that you could ever aspire to, Temple," she said coolly, then looked at Nash. "Tell Lisa I'll call her tonight."

Temple watched her go, his gaze raking over her like a man starved for a look, Nash thought, then whistled softly.

"I'd stay away from that fire if I were you, Temp. Hell, I thought you two could at least be friends." Temple and Hope had dated for two years and no one knew what split them apart. Neither would tell.

"For Hope, there's no gray area."

Nash just shook his head. "I gotta go."

Temple looked at him. "Anything I can help with?"

"Yeah. Stop by Kate's and tell her Lisa's shop is closed."

Nash handed him the address. Temple glanced at it. "Why? There's already a sign on the door."

Nash frowned. Suddenly he took the slip of paper, pitched his coffee and headed to his car.

NASH STARED down at the reports, then started writing each item down on an index card. Soon he had a hundred cards covering his desk.

"What the hell are you doing, Couviyon?" Jack Walker said, strolling up to his desk.

"Detective work, maybe you remember it?"

Jack Walker smirked.

"I was hoping this could help." Nash shrugged. "Winfield and Chartres die of poison, but Chartres got a little arsenic. From peach pits, no less."

"A nature-loving killer?"

"No, I don't think so. The bath tea that killed Winfield wasn't sealed correctly. Our killer didn't know how. Chartres and Delan were together against Winfield, but Winfield roped in Delan with riches. She liked sleeping with a married man—she was a hooker once. Needed excitement and danger, I guess." He shrugged again, taking away cards as he spoke. "But I bet when Winfield learned what she was up to, he dumped her. He was a stickler for appearances and Delan wasn't in his class. Then he tried to get Lisa back. And he'd planned on using property to do it." Nash took away another card.

Hope strolled in, saying hi to the officers, then stopped at Nash's desk. "Our city is in for some setbacks if this is how you solve crimes, Detective."

"Looking mighty fine there, Randall," Jack said, giving her the once-over.

She brought her gaze to his, smiling, and Nash could have sworn she actually blushed. "Thank you, Sheriff. Lose any parolees?"

"Not this week. They're afraid of you coming after them, so they stay put."

Nash glanced between the two, thinking of Temple, then gave it up. His brother was too much of a player for Hope.

"Quinn asked me to give this to you," Hope said, handing him a thin file just as an officer hurried over to Nash and laid another down before walking away.

"It's about time," Nash said, then opened the background reports first.

"Can I help?" Hope asked. "I want this killer caught, too. Lisa's having just too many bad-hair days because of it."

Nash chuckled. "Have a look." He eased back in the chair, reading the file on Peter Winfield.

While Hope leaned over the cards, Nash flipped through credit reports and found large sums deposited from a New Orleans bank a couple of years ago, which confirmed the blackmail. Credit cards used at clubs and restaurants and a few newspaper clippings were also in the file. One clipping showed Winfield at a fund-raiser with a woman. Nash took out a magnifying glass, but the photo was grainy and the woman's face was turned away as if she was talking to someone behind her. Right height for Delan, he thought. The information fed through his brain like ticker tape. He reached for the forensic report.

"Chartres is eliminated for obvious reasons. He was dying of poison when Lisa was attacked," Nash said. "But the unanswered question is, why was Winfield killed?"

"Not for money—Lisa gets it," Jack said. "It stays in probate with the will. No one can touch it."

"It's passion, revenge," Nash said. "The destroyed apartment was the killer venting. The killer got calm in the bedroom and carefully laid out the gown. Then stabbed it."

"And the killer's angry that Lisa hasn't been charged, too," Jack added. "Which is likely the reason behind the attack in her house."

The phone shrilled and Nash snatched it up. NYPD Detective Rhinehart was on the other end. "I'm faxing you the forensic reports on the hair found in the apartment," Rhinehart said.

"Hallelujah." Nash glanced over as the fax machine hummed and spit out the paper. He grabbed it, then flipped open Quinn's analysis and slid out the one for the hairs found at the inn.

"It matches our sample." The hairs were from a female and chemically lightened.

"Yeah, now to match it with a head."

"Not Kathy Boon and not Lisa." Nash told Rhinehart about the attack on Lisa.

Rhinehart admitted to being stumped. Every suspect

had a motive, and Delan and Chartres had time and opportunity. Chartres was dead, a great eliminator.

"Catherine Delan is out on bail, Nash."

"What! For how long?"

"Two days. We have no evidence that she killed Winfield, only that she was sleeping with him. Covering up blackmail is low on the list here, you know?"

"Yeah, thanks." As he hung up, Nash's gaze swept over photos, then he slipped suspect statements from a file.

"Is this evidence?" Hope pointed to the bags. Nash nodded, reading. Hope opened the largest bag, the one containing Peter Winfield's clothing, and when she held up the green shirt a distinct odor came with it.

"Let me see that," Nash said. She handed it to him. "This was the shirt he was wearing when he met with Lisa." He inhaled the scent. "I've smelled that before."

"Aftershave?" Jack said, sniffing.

Hope shook her head. "Too many high notes."

Nash reared back in his chair, and Walker simply folded his arms, waiting for an explanation.

Hope blushed a little. "Perfumes have high and low notes, part of the scents that make up perfume. Spice, flowers, musk. It's the combination of these and the level of the notes that make one perfume different from others." She put her wrist under Nash's nose and he got a whiff. "No flowers, no musk, only spice."

Walker smiled crookedly. "Wise choice."

She tipped her nose up. "It's custom-made."

"Lisa's scent is jasmine." Nash slipped the scarf free of the bag. Walker inhaled, as did Hope.

"This—" she tapped the victim's shirt "—is high flowers and musk."

Nash phoned Quinn to ask about the smell on Winfield's shirt.

"I couldn't get the exact mix to define it," Quinn said. "It was the only garment with the scent on it. Sweet flowers and musk, but I'm still trying. Just wish my memory was better."

"Why?"

"Because I've smelled it before, outside the lab. I can't recall where."

Nash asked him another couple of questions, then redialed Rhinehart to ask him about odors in the clothing. There were none, so that meant Winfield got it here in Indigo.

Nash stared out the window, ignoring the world.

"I can hear the wheels turning in your head," Hope said to him. "Speak."

"Not yet. But do me a favor—check out these people." He slipped the list of names free and handed it to her, then he jotted something on another slip of paper. "Ask if they saw this person between ten and midnight."

"My services will cost you."

Scooping up his index cards, Nash said, "The sheriff is good for it."

Walker winked at Hope, and she smiled as she left the police station. Nash headed out, too. He had something he had to do. Right now. He'd waited four years too long to start living and wasn't wasting a second more. Not even with a killer on the loose.

NASH FOUND Lisa snoozing in the solarium on an old sofa. Sitting on the edge of the sofa, he kissed her awake and slid a ring onto her finger.

Lisa inhaled and sat up. "Nash."

"Will you marry me?" he asked, down on one knee.

Tears sprang from her eyes and she cupped his jaw and kissed him. Her lip quivered and Nash drank in her sobs.

"Please say yes, Lisa. I spent an hour picking that out, and you need to say yes and put me out of my misery, or just shoot me."

She smiled, pulling him down to her. "Yes, yes. Oh, yes!"

Nash kissed her deeply, madly, and had his hand up her shirt when someone behind them cleared their throat. He pressed his forehead to hers, catching his breath before leaning back to look at his oldest brother.

"You sure know how to spoil a moment, Logan."

It was Lisa who said it, making Nash smile.

Logan's gaze lowered to her hand, and his smile was faint and a little envious.

"Congratulations, little brother. And forgive me." Logan crossed to Lisa, drawing her from the couch and kissing her cheek. "Welcome to the family." He shook his brother's hand. "I really hate to interrupt, but Hope Randall is on the phone."

"Hope?" Lisa asked.

"She was checking something out for me. Pray she found it." Nash squeezed Lisa's hand and hurried to the phone in the hall.

Logan stared at Lisa. "Thank you for tending to Mother."

"You're welcome. She's a lovely woman."

"She was."

"No, Logan, she still is and will be again. When we find the killer."

"We've been hunting for a while now."

"You can't give up."

"I don't think I know how." He was quiet, staring at the plant-filled room. Sunlight spilled from the glass ceiling, draping him in white light, and Lisa thought she'd never seen anyone as formidable as Logan Davis Couviyon. Nor as unapproachable. Then she remembered that he had the burden of the plantation, the lumber and mill businesses the Couviyon family owned, which employed half the town.

"You hate it here?" Lisa asked.

"No, of course not."

"You were raised to take over for your father, Logan. Is that what you want?"

His shoulders drooped and he shoved his fingers through his hair. It was the first time she'd ever seen him look mussed.

"I don't really know anymore."

"Maybe it's time you found out what would actually put a smile on your face. It is a handsome face when you manage to not look like you're about to chew leather."

His features tightened.

"More than you wanted to hear?" she said.

"Apparently." Logan smiled sheepishly, and it did amazing things for his features. "You're going to be a welcome addition around here, Lisa."

She wasn't going to tell him that she had no intention of moving in and starting her marriage with Nash under the nose of his family. But Logan was a brooding man and lonely, too, though he'd never admit it.

"You might live to regret that."

He smiled.

"You know, Logan, you really need to wear something else besides button-down shirts and slacks. This is your house, not the office. And maybe a little color?"

Logan looked down at his white shirt and black slacks. "I'm used to it."

"Repeat after me, 'Change is good.'"

He laughed softly. "I shall."

"Shall? See there. How about saying okay or fine?"

Nash popped back in long enough to kiss Lisa goodbye. "I'm sorry, baby, I have to leave." He hurried to the door. "Stay put."

Lisa sighed and looked down at the diamond ring on her hand.

''Crime fighting is hell on a relationship, huh?'' Logan said.

Lisa watched Nash tear out the door, and she just smiled.

HOPE'S CALL had given him another piece to the puzzle. One more person had opportunity—he just didn't know the motive. Didn't have a solid connection. Nash drove, the windows closed and the air conditioner turned up. The scent of Winfield's shirt filled his cruiser, and after a few moments, he remembered where he'd smelled it.

Lisa will be furious, he thought, and for a second her face, the instant he'd slipped the ring on her finger, materialized in his mind. He was lucky she was going to marry him, he thought; then a second later his features tightened as the puzzle fell into place. Pulling the car off the road, he accessed his police computer, doing a search on state marriage licenses issued in the past two months.

As the screen blinked up, Nash grinned.

Gotcha.

Chapter Thirteen

Lisa saw a figure come around from the side of the house, and while Olivia was down on her knees pulling weeds and dropping them into a basket, Lisa shielded her eyes to look at the newcomer. "Oh, hi, Kate. What are you doing here?"

"I tried to call, but the number's unlisted."

Lisa smiled at the house, then Kate. "I know. The shop's closed until the doors are repaired."

"There's a locksmith and carpenter at the shop. I was driving by and saw them."

"Really?" Nash must have called them to fix the doors, Lisa thought. "Was anyone else there?"

"No. Want to take a ride over and see what they're up to?" Kate asked, her gaze shifting to Olivia, then to the house. "Man, this place is huge."

"Be glad neither of us has to clean it."

Kate smiled. "Who's the lady?"

Lisa glanced back at the older woman. "Olivia Couviyon. Nash's mother."

Kate frowned softly. ''I heard talk about her. Isn't she a little cra—''

Lisa sent Kate a hard look.

''Sorry. So, you want to go to the shop and see what these guys are doing or let them just fix it?''

Lisa didn't want men working in her house or shop without someone there. But she'd promised Nash she'd remain at Indigo Run. ''Let me make a couple of calls.''

''Sure. But I just saw a guy in a black sports car drive away from here.''

That must have been Logan, Lisa thought. ''Just the same, come on with me.''

''No problem.''

Lisa went to Olivia, whispering softly that she was going out for a while. Olivia nodded, her focus on the weeds. Lisa noticed that this particular rosebush had no weeds to speak of, and the mulched area around it was perfect, the edges clean. Not that the rest wasn't well tended, but this spot was perfect.

Lisa really didn't want to leave Olivia alone, and she decided to ask MaryGrace to keep an eye on her. She walked into the house, Kate behind her.

She called for MaryGrace. When she didn't get an answer, she went to the nearest phone and dialed Nash. She got his office voice mail and left a message for him to call her, then dialed his pager. Concerned that MaryGrace didn't seem to be around, Lisa said to Kate, ''I'll just be a second.'' Then she headed deeper into the house. ''Meet me at the front door.''

"Certainly."

Lisa's steps faltered and she glanced back. How odd that Kate had answered the same way Peter always had, she thought. Lisa called for MaryGrace as Kate went to the front-door foyer.

"MaryGrace?" Not finding her in the kitchen, Lisa trotted up the staircase, opening door after door. MaryGrace was nowhere to be found. "I guess she went to the grocery store," Lisa muttered to herself, going back downstairs and walking toward Logan's office.

Kate stepped close. "We should be going. I hate to think of those people in your shop with access into the house."

That was true, Lisa thought, moving just inside the doorway to Logan's office. It was empty, too. Okay, something's wrong. Logan would never have left here if MaryGrace was gone too.

"That guy who left in the black car. He looks like your detective," Kate said.

"Yes, that's Logan, Nash's brother."

Lisa got a creepy feeling, from the empty house, from Kate, from the whole situation. Kate was looking at her carefully, as if measuring her against something.

"You okay?" she asked Kate.

"Yeah, fine. Just concerned."

Lisa glanced around, the silence of the house eerie. She listened to her gut instinct. "Look, Kate. I better not leave. If the craftsmen do anything wrong, then they'll have to pay for it. Can you stop by and tell them to stop their work till they talk with me?'' Lisa stepped farther into the office, her gaze moving over the desk for a note.

''I can't do that,'' Kate said.

''Why not? You live two streets over.''

''You need to come with me, Lisa.''

Lisa twisted to look behind her and found herself staring down the barrel of a gun.

A DOZEN OFFICERS surrounded the little house owned by Kate Holling, and when the bullhorns didn't bring a response, the SWAT team spilled in through the back doors. ''Clear'' repeated like a chant. After getting the nod, Nash prepared to kick open the front door.

The explosion ripped the door off its hinges and sent Nash flying backward down the steps. He hit the sidewalk hard, his gun spinning from his hand.

LISA LIFTED her gaze from the weapon to Kate. ''You?''

Kate smirked to herself. ''Good, aren't I?''

''Why?'' Lisa inched back against the edge of the desk behind her.

''Paying you back.''

''For what?''

''For keeping Peter stuck on you when it was me he was supposed to marry.''

''Why would he marry you?''

It was the wrong thing to say. Kate's expression turned black with rage and her voice rose.

"Because I loved him! You had your chance."

This wasn't making any sense to Lisa. But the gun did. She looked around for something to defend herself with.

Kate moved closer. "Don't even think about it."

"Where are Logan and MaryGrace?" Lisa took a step back and her foot hit something soft. She looked down and saw a hand. Logan was under the desk, unconscious, his head bleeding. "Oh, God." She reached for him, but Kate pushed the gun barrel into her back.

"Back off, Lisa."

Lisa stilled. "He's bleeding."

"Good. If I'm lucky it'll keep going till he's dead. Come on. I prefer to do this in private." Kate flicked the gun barrel in the direction of the door.

"How did you know Peter?"

"I worked for him, in New York. Now get moving."

"Not till you tell me why you killed Peter."

"I thought it was obvious. Because he still loved you. He had Catherine Delan and he still wanted you." Every time Kate said "you," she brought the gun closer to Lisa's head. "He had me, and he still kept talking about you." Kate nudged Lisa's head with the muzzle. "I was sick of it."

Lisa gaped. "You were jealous?"

Kate's expression soured. "No, I was pissed off.

Killing him wasn't the point. The point was setting you up to take the fall.''

''What the hell did I ever do to you?'' Lisa asked.

''We've been over this, *Mrs. Winfield*. You had a hold on him that no one could break.''

''That's because he couldn't have me, Kate.'' Lisa hoped to reason with her, but it was hopeless. Kate was in another dimension. With a gun.

''He wasn't supposed to die,'' Kate said. ''Well, not till the next day, anyway. The fool went and used the tea in the tub. When I came to see him, he was already dying.''

''The basket the police found. You took one from the shop?'' Lisa was certain she wasn't missing one. And it told her Kate had planned this for a long time. She'd applied for a job so she could kill her.

''No, I had a friend buy one when I got to this town. Get moving, Lisa. Trying to mess with my head will only get you killed sooner.''

Lisa swallowed and obeyed, walking out of the study. Kate seemed calm and controlled. Like Peter. And Peter always snapped eventually.

''Whatever you're planning won't work.'' Lisa stopped in the hall.

''Really? I confess, I did it,'' Kate said dramatically. ''I couldn't live with myself and deceive the people I loved.'' Her expression hardened. ''That's what the letter you're going to write will say.''

''A confession letter?'' Lisa said. ''No one would ever believe it. There're too many people involved.

You killed Chartres and you tried to choke me to death.''

"None of this would have happened if you'd just drunk the tea I made you," Kate said.

The night she'd returned from New York, Lisa realized. The meal, the tea on the stove. "You know all they have to do is check flights you took to get here."

Kate's features tightened as the realization set in. Her timing was off.

Lisa noticed. "You were the one in the black coat at the funeral. You destroyed the apartment, the nightgown. The one who hit me on the head." Lisa hadn't thought to check to see if the shop had been opened and Kate was there. Lisa hadn't arrived home till late. Kate could have easily left New York and returned to Indigo before her. "Attacking me in my home was your worst mistake. It proved I was being set up."

"You should have been in jail!"

"I'm innocent. I'm not going anywhere. Nash is probably on his way," Lisa said.

"Your white knight isn't coming. Right about now, he should be dead."

NASH BLINKED and rolled as debris rained down on him and the other officers. The wail of fire-truck sirens grew louder.

Jack Walker rushed to him, pulling him back from the flames. Acrid vapor billowed.

"Anyone hurt?" Nash asked when he got to his

feet, coughing hard and bracing his hands on his knees.

Walker shook his head. "Not too bad. SWAT team was already coming out."

Nash and Walker shouted into the radio for their fellow officers and rushed to the side of the house. The fire trucks pulled up and firefighters spilled out, rushing to douse the flames. Nash and Walker pulled one man out and away from the fire, then helped him to the ambulance.

"Good God," Nash said, staring at the house and sagging against his cruiser. Firefighters quickly controlled the blaze and kept it from spreading to nearby homes.

"Kate wasn't coming back. Not with that explosion," Nash said, and started moving to the car door. Lisa. Oh, God.

"It only destroyed the front of the house."

A firefighter, his face black with soot, rushed to catch Nash. "Hey, Detective, this yours?" He slapped the pager into Nash's hand.

Nash smirked at it. It was humming. "Must be broken," he said, rubbing the dirt off the cracked glass and reading the numbers. As realization set in, he felt sick with fear. Lisa. At Indigo Run.

LISA'S EYES widened, and panic drained the blood from her face. "What did you do?"

Kate said nothing, pushing Lisa toward the front door.

"What did you do!" she demanded, turning on Kate.

"I killed him."

Lisa's knees went soft and she gripped the door frame. No, she thought. Nash wasn't dead. He couldn't be. Anger crushed her and Lisa wanted to tear Kate in two. And her expression said as much. Kate took a step back, aiming the gun.

Suddenly the phone rang. Lisa looked at it, then Kate. "They will know something's wrong if I don't answer it."

Kate walked over to the phone, lifted the receiver. The instant she did, Lisa screamed for help, but just as quickly, Kate set it back down again.

"Nice try." She shoved Lisa out the front door and onto the porch.

"Where are we going?"

"You're going to hell. I'm going to the Cayman Islands and live the life of Reilly with Peter's money."

"You can't imagine you'll get out of the country after all you've done."

Kate snickered, thinking that Lisa didn't know what Peter had really been like. "I'm a whiz with computers, just like Peter. And he had more cash than God. A lot more. He stashed it in off shore banks. He and Forsythe had been double-dealing in the stock market."

"The police know about that. The accounts will be seized if they haven't been already," Lisa said.

The news didn't change Kate's expression. "Not in Grand Cayman, they won't."

"So you think you'll get out of the country to enjoy it?"

Smiling thinly, Kate looked over at Lisa, and Lisa understood that Kate could somehow use her as a hostage or shield to get away.

"Chartres saw you, didn't he?"

"Yeah, he found the basket. I'd stashed it that day in the linen closet. The idiot never went up there, but that night he did. He saw me on the back balcony, too, so he said. When the police learned he'd lied, he said if I didn't pay him to keep quiet, he'd turn me in. He didn't get the chance."

"They found your hair in the inn, Kate. They can make a match. DNA is a powerful tool. Killing me will get you nothing."

"Maybe, maybe not."

"Forensics is too good—they'll know it was murder. Blood patterns, residue on the hands. They'll know. Just like they know Chartres was murdered."

Kate waved, her expression sour. "Shut up. At least you'll be dead."

"You were stupid. The last thing you should have used was herbs and flowers. The trail came to me, but it was too tidy. And I'm not that dumb," Lisa said.

"Oh, yeah? That's not what Peter said."

Kate shoved Lisa down the front steps, using the gun to nudge her toward Logan's car. Lisa noticed that

MaryGrace's car was still in the carriage house. "You won't get the insurance, either."

"I would have if I'd been married to him at the time." Kate opened Logan's car door and tossed Lisa the keys she must have taken off the desk. "Get in."

Lisa refused to move. Kate grabbed Lisa's blouse and pushed her into the car.

Lisa kicked Kate in the knee and pushed herself out of the car. "I'm not leaving here with you. And what did you do to MaryGrace? Where is she?"

Kate rolled to the side, cocking the pistol hammer and pointing. "Give it up, Lisa, and worry about what I'll do to the old woman…" Kate swung the weapon to the right—where Olivia was strolling in their direction, periodically stopping to take a rose cutting.

Renewed fury filled Lisa. "Leave her out of this."

"Then you come with me now."

Lisa knew if she left this house with Kate, there would be no hope for her. "No."

Kate aimed at Olivia, who was blissfully unaware of the danger a short distance away.

Lisa dove for the gun. Kate pulled the trigger, the shot deafening. Olivia screamed and Kate backhanded Lisa, cutting her lip and sending her stumbling back against the car. Then Kate grabbed her hair and dragged her over to the old woman. She pushed Lisa to the ground.

Olivia stared blankly between the two women. Lisa wanted Olivia to run, but knew Kate would shoot the woman in the back. She'd already killed two people. One more wouldn't make a difference to her.

"This will be better," Kate said. "She's crazy—the whole town talks about her. She was the witness to a murder and who's to say she didn't kill her husband?"

Kate pointed the gun at Lisa.

Olivia blinked between the two. "You're Temple's new girlfriend?"

"Shut up."

"Why, darlin', come in and have some lemonade while we wait for him. He's still at his classes."

Lisa's gaze shot to Olivia and she wondered if the woman was lucid or still in her own world. Lisa tried to stand.

Kate shoved her back down. "Stay there. I like you in the dirt. Every time I saw those clothes in your closet, the jewelry Peter never gave me—"

"Peter was a user, Kate. He didn't know how to love anyone." Lisa caught movement in the corner of her eye. Olivia was reaching into her apron pocket.

"You really should come in out of this heat, dear." Olivia said to Kate. "It's not good for your complexion."

"Shut up!" Kate kept her eyes on Lisa. "No, don't move. I like that frightened-deer look. You wear it well. Stay down!"

"But then, you could wear a hat. Yes, you should wear a hat. You have freckles," Olivia said.

Kate's gaze jerked briefly to the old woman. "Shut up, you crazy old bat!"

Olivia moved toward a bush and nearer to Lisa. "Would you like some roses? I have the best in the county. There isn't another garden that has this rose."

"Lady, I swear," Kate said.

Olivia's gaze snapped to the gun as if seeing it for the first time, and she dropped the garden shears, stepping back. "No, no, don't! I'll give them to you! All of them!"

While Kate was distracted by Olivia, Lisa grabbed the sheers and plunged them into Kate's thigh.

Her scream pierced the damp air, and Lisa jumped to her feet, pushing Olivia out of the way. Kate yanked at the shears buried in her thigh, the gun faltering. Lisa's fist connected with Kate's jaw and pain rang up her arm. A second later Lisa went for the gun.

But Kate lifted her arm and a shot rang out.

Lisa lurched back, looking down at herself, then at Kate. Blood fountained from Kate's shoulder. Her finger was still on the trigger. The hammer was still cocked. She hadn't fired.

Nash rushed up, knocking the gun from Kate's hand and pushing Lisa behind him. Then with his foot he clipped Kate behind the knees and she dropped to the ground with a howl of pain. In seconds Nash had Kate cuffed and facedown in the dirt. He turned to Lisa.

She stared at him, her vision blurring.

"You going to faint?" he asked. She looked pale.

She latched on to him, holding tightly. "Don't be ridiculous. A case of the vapors is so passé." He closed his arms around her and she began to cry, tension releasing with each tear. "Thank you."

He rubbed her spine. "It's okay, baby, you're safe. We're all safe." She clung tighter, her face buried in his shirtfront. "Now you have to marry me, Lisa. You owe me."

She chuckled, then tipped her head back and met his gaze. He kissed her deeply, his own fears seeping from him with each touch of her mouth. He'd been terrified on his way here, terrified he'd find her gone or, worse, dead. Nash had never before driven so fast and recklessly. Because his entire life was at the end of this road.

Suddenly Lisa broke the kiss. "Your mother!" Lisa tore from his arms and they rushed to where Olivia lay on the ground.

The old woman brushed off their helping hands and sat up. "I'm fine. I really must keep my eye out for tree roots," she said, then smiled at Lisa and Nash. "I'm always tripping on them." She looked at her son. "I see you put a ring on her finger. Smartened up a bit, didn't you, Nash?"

Nash chuckled and looked at Lisa as Indigo Run Plantation filled with sirens and police cars.

"Took me a while, but yes, ma'am, I did."

Olivia stood, patted his arm, then trotted off, muttering, "Good, good."

"I think she approves," Nash said. "But it wouldn't matter, anyway."

Lisa arched a brow, smiling. "Save a life and you

go and get all defiant.'' She tisked softly. ''And to your mama, no less.''

Nash hugged her, pressing his lips to her temple and acknowledging how close he'd come to losing her. And how lucky he was to have her in his arms, making wisecracks.

When Kate muttered something about wanting Lisa to still pay, Nash led Lisa away. The uniformed officers took charge.

APART FROM a bruised shoulder, from being pushed into the pantry by Kate, MaryGrace was unharmed. She complained to Logan that there should be a light-switch inside the pantry and maybe air-conditioning. She was suffering from the heat when Nash found her. Logan was treated for his head injury and refused, in typical Couviyon fashion, Lisa thought, to go to the hospital.

''You yelled at me and insisted I go. Why not him?'' Lisa asked.

''He's stubborn and I love you more.''

As the EMT put a stitch in Logan's head, Logan glanced up and smiled.

''How did you know, Nash? I didn't,'' Lisa said. Since Kate had confessed to Lisa, Lisa gave a statement and would have to testify later.

''Aside from the fact that the hair matched—brown hair bleached to blond but didn't match Delan's—and that Catherine Delan was free on bail, I had to think, who could get close to you and do that to your doors, get the lock out of the wood. And to know when and where you were all the time. The scent on Peter's clothes, well, Quinn and I both recognized it from somewhere other than Winfield's clothing. Quinn had taken Kate out and had been that close to her. Then there was the marriage license.''

"Peter was actually going to marry Kate? She's so not his type.''

"Was anyone? There was a license issued to her with Peter's name on it. I don't think he ever intended to marry her. She did the paperwork.''

"How did you think to look for it?''

"I was thinking about you, the look on your face when I proposed and…well, things just multiplied in my mind.''

Her look encouraged him to explain. "I want to marry you, soon, and I thought the first thing we need is a license." She smiled softly. "So checking licenses issued in the last few months was a hunch. I figured if Winfield used one woman, he'd used more to get what he wanted. I had to understand why Winfield was killed, and it was for love. It had to be enough to orchestrate this murder. Framing you was paying back the one person she blamed for not getting what she wanted. The killer had to get close enough to you to have access to your house, the shop and herbs. Catherine Delan didn't love Peter, plus she was out on bail, but didn't leave New York. Her hair didn't match the strands found in the apartment or the bedding. The only person who could get close enough to you was

Kate. I had Hope check out the list of people Kate gave me who'd seen Kate at the club the night of Peter's murder. She was missing at the time when you were in that hotel room. She had to have been on the back balcony listening and waiting until you left to leave the basket behind. I'd bet she came back to put the scarf on Winfield's neck and make certain he was dead or near dead. Her hair was bleached, too. We'll get a match, I'm sure. But when I asked Temple to put up a closed sign at your shop after the attack, I'd realized she lived only a couple streets from your house, and ran right home after attacking you. That's when I started making the connections to her.''

"She said she had someone buy the basket from me months before she came for a job. And that Chartres saw her put the basket in the storage closet and also saw her on the back balcony. He blackmailed her.''

That's why he looked so smug that day in the hotel, Nash realized. He'd been hiding a killer so he could recoup his loses. It got him killed. "Her hair and prints will probably show up in Chartres's place. She knew we were close. She'd rigged her house with a bomb to destroy any evidence.''

Lisa shivered, knowing how close she came to losing Nash.

She hugged him, his strength and warmth seeping into her and erasing any remnant of the terror Kate had instilled in her. "Your mother, how is she?''

"In the cottage as if nothing happened.''

"She saved my life, Nash.'' Lisa gripped his arms.

"She knew we were in danger. She knew to drop those shears near enough for me to reach."

"Lisa, I don't think that's the case," Logan said. "She was just doing what she wanted."

Lisa shook her head, her gaze pinning him. "You're wrong, Logan. You all are," she said, her gaze stopping on each member of the family. "Olivia isn't lost. She knows. She just doesn't want to let anyone else know."

"Not even us?" Logan said, resentment in his tone.

Lisa's shoulders lifted and fell. "Did you ever think that maybe, locked in that world of hers, she's protecting all of you?"

"Finally," MaryGrace said, pushing herself off the living-room chair and moving to Lisa. She hugged her quickly and fiercely, then looked at the men. "Haven't I been telling you boys that? Haven't I?"

"Yes, MaryGrace," Temple, Nash and Logan said together.

MaryGrace pushed a lock of hair off Lisa's forehead, then kissed her there. "Thank you, honey, thank you." When she leaned back, Lisa felt a tear roll down her cheek. She and MaryGrace had their own idea about reaching Olivia, even if the brothers were too stubborn to see it.

"Lisa, come on upstairs and have a bath. Wash off that evil woman's—"

"Cooties?" Nash said.

MaryGrace hid her smile, but Lisa laughed out loud. She could do that now. She wasn't in danger. Kate was behind bars, and she was about to start her life with Nash. Ascending the stairs with MaryGrace, Lisa stopped at the landing to look down at Nash.

He stood at the base watching her, one hand on the handcarved newel-post, his brothers flanking him as they looked up at her. The police, forensic team and EMTs moved about doing their jobs.

"I love you, Lisa Bracket," Nash said and his voice held the tender need she'd longed to hear for years.

She smiled, her heart skipping a beat, then drumming hard. "And I love you, Nash Couviyon."

"You're going to marry me."

"Oh, yeah."

"And we're going to fill this house with babies and laughter."

Her expression brightened. "Won't your brothers be jealous?"

Nash didn't look at his siblings. "We'll just have to help them find what we have."

MaryGrace rushed back to the railing and shouted down, "If anyone's doing the matchmaking around here, Nash Couviyon, it's going to be me. I diapered your behinds. It's my right."

Temple groaned, Logan smirked as if he'd never worn a diaper and Nash simply grinned and winked at the housekeeper.

"Yes, ma'am."

After a second the Couviyons burst with laughter.

Nash looked around at his family, then at the woman he loved. Lisa brought more than happiness to

Nash. She gave hope to his family. Hope that the doors of Indigo Run were opening again, just waiting for more love and laughter to sweep inside and save their souls.

* * * * *

Next month look for
Amy J. Fetzer's Silhouette Desire,
AWAKENING BEAUTY.

HARLEQUIN®
INTRIGUE®

has a new lineup of books to keep you on the edge of your seat throughout the winter. So be on the alert for...

BACHELORS AT LARGE

Bold and brash—these men have sworn to serve and protect as officers of the law...and only the most special women can "catch" these good guys!

UNDER HIS PROTECTION
BY AMY J. FETZER
(October 2003)

UNMARKED MAN
BY DARLENE SCALERA
(November 2003)

BOYS IN BLUE
A special 3-in-1 volume with
REBECCA YORK (Ruth Glick writing as Rebecca York),
ANN VOSS PETERSON AND PATRICIA ROSEMOOR
(December 2003)

CONCEALED WEAPON
BY SUSAN PETERSON
(January 2004)

GUARDIAN OF HER HEART
BY LINDA O. JOHNSTON
(February 2004)

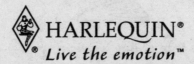

HARLEQUIN®
® *Live the emotion*™

**Visit us at www.eHarlequin.com
and www.tryintrigue.com**

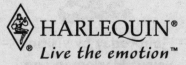

If you enjoyed what you just read,
then we've got an offer you can't resist!

Take 2 bestselling
love stories FREE!
Plus get a FREE surprise gift!

Clip this page and mail it to Harlequin Reader Service

IN U.S.A.
3010 Walden Ave.
P.O. Box 1867
Buffalo, N.Y. 14240-1867

IN CANADA
P.O. Box 609
Fort Erie, Ontario
L2A 5X3

YES! Please send me 2 free Harlequin Intrigue® novels and my free surprise gift. After receiving them, if I don't wish to receive anymore, I can return the shipping statement marked cancel. If I don't cancel, I will receive 6 brand-new novels each month, before they're available in stores! In the U.S.A., bill me at the bargain price of $3.99 plus 25¢ shipping and handling per book and applicable sales tax, if any*. In Canada, bill me at the bargain price of $4.74 plus 25¢ shipping and handling per book and applicable taxes**. That's the complete price and a savings of at least 10% off the cover prices—what a great deal! I understand that accepting the 2 free books and gift places me under no obligation ever to buy any books. I can always return a shipment and cancel at any time. Even if I never buy another book from Harlequin, the 2 free books and gift are mine to keep forever.

182 HDN DU9K
382 HDN DU9L

Name	(PLEASE PRINT)	
Address	Apt.#	
City	State/Prov.	Zip/Postal Code

* Terms and prices subject to change without notice. Sales tax applicable in N.Y.
** Canadian residents will be charged applicable provincial taxes and GST.
  All orders subject to approval. Offer limited to one per household and not valid to
  current Harlequin Intrigue® subscribers.
  ® are registered trademarks of Harlequin Enterprises Limited.

INT03

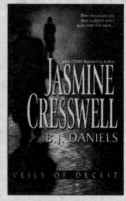